ROOM WITH A CLUE

...rkley Prime Crime Book / published by arrangement with
the author

PRINTING HISTORY
Jove edition / September 1993
Berkley Prime Crime edition / September 1993

ISBN: 0-425-14326-0

Berkley Prime Crime Books are published by
The Berkley Publishing Group,
200 Madison Avenue, New York, New York 10016.
The name BERKLEY PRIME CRIME and the
...KLEY PRIME CRIME design are trademarks belonging to
Berkley Publishing Corporation.

PRINTED IN THE UNITED STATES OF AMERICA

10 9 8 7 6 5 4 3 2

W9-BCA-629

No hint of scandal ever touched the name of the
Pennyfoot. Though the staff might gossip, as indeed they
did, no word had ever been leaked outside the hotel
walls. Their jobs depended on it. The success of the hotel
depended on it.

All that was about to change, Cecily thought, as she
followed Baxter and John Thimble into the courtyard.
The flickering light from the hurricane lamps illuminated
the scene.

Her mind seemed to register the tiniest details, as if
needing to implant them for posterity. Chunks from the
roof garden wall had gouged the surface of the courtyard
floor. The scent of roses mingled with the earthy odor of
clean, damp soil, seeming somehow appropriate for the
smell of death. She tilted her head back slowly, reluctant
to confirm what she already knew. Against the darkening
sky, the ugly gap in the outline of the wall was a stark
accusation of her own negligence. If only she'd spotted
the damage earlier. It could have been repaired by now.
A woman's death would not then lie heavy on her
conscience.

Thunder rolled in the distance from the dying storm.
Some feet from where the men struggled to lift the
lifeless body off the jagged rocks, a pitiful pile of
uprooted edelweiss tangled with a yellow rock
rose . . .

SPECIAL PREVIEW!

Turn to the back for an intriguing look
at the further adventures of Cecily Sinclair
In Do Not Disturb,
the second Pennyfoot Hotel mystery
By Kate Kingsbury

A PENNYFOOT HOT

ROOM
A CL

KATE KING

Peabody Public
Columbia City

BERKLEY PRIME CRIME,

If you
book i
publish
payme

A B

b
P

BER

CHAPTER

1

The British subjects had grown accustomed to their warm Edwardian summers, and the cool, damp season of 1906 came as rather a disappointment.

A sudden squall in the English Channel dumped a measure of rain on the southeast coast that evening in mid-June, soaking the thatched roofs of the cottages in Badgers End and leaving puddles in the courtyard of the Pennyfoot Hotel.

Not long after the storm had passed, a shadowy figure paused at the wall of the hotel roof garden and looked down on the deserted Esplanade. The wind felt cold and damp, and few would be inclined to brave a late night stroll along the sands in such weather.

After furtively looking around, the figure crouched and stretched out a hand with a long, thin knife in its grasp. With swift, short jabs, the knife chipped away at the aged mortar that

1

bound the bricks, finding little resistance in the dry, crumbling texture.

The hand worked steadily at the wall, until an area roughly three feet wide and four feet deep had been gouged and weakened. Then the figure rose and on silent feet faded into the shadows.

The following morning Cecily Sinclair was late for the meeting to organize the Friday ball. Her two committee members were constantly at loggerheads, and it usually took all her considerable powers of diplomacy to avoid a confrontation. So it was with some trepidation that she entered the hotel library.

Phoebe Carter-Holmes was outspoken, to say the least, and made no secret about her disapproval of Madeline Pengrath. When Cecily hurried through the large paneled doors, she heard Phoebe's shrill voice declare, "Upon my word, Madeline, I've never heard such utter nonsense in my entire life."

Cecily took her seat at the head of the heavy Jacobean table and frowned at Phoebe. "And what is it that you are dismissing as such nonsense?"

Phoebe waved a gloved hand in irritation. "She's muttering all that mumbo jumbo again. I don't know what possesses her to dally in that sinful rubbish."

Cecily was very fond of Madeline. That didn't mean that she believed all the drivel the villagers whispered about her. After all, Cecily prided herself on her common sense. As the only girl in a family of six, her brothers had instilled in her an inquisitive mind and a zest for adventure, and recognizing the futility of control, her mother had taken great pains to ensure her daughter kept a realistic outlook on the world.

Most of the villagers in Badgers End were convinced that Madeline was a gypsy changeling. "Talks to the animals, she does, and they understand every blooming word she says," they whispered to each other when she passed by. "Don't matter whether it be animals, birds, or plants, they knows exactly what she's saying to 'em."

Well, maybe the plants stretched it a bit, but the woman definitely had "powers." For one thing, she never seemed to get any older. Neither the icy winter winds that blew in from

the English Channel nor the midsummer sun that bleached
Lord Withersgill's wheat fields appeared to mar Madeline's
smooth skin.

She always wore her long dark hair floating about her
shoulders. Her bean-pole figure was invariably enveloped in
soft muslin, which swirled around her like a captured cloud.
When seen gliding across the croquet lawn in the gathering
dusk, she looked rather like a benevolent ghost on a mission.

The petite woman made Cecily feel big and clumsy. She
tried not to envy the long, gleaming black tresses that showed
none of the gray hairs that sprinkled profusely through her own
light brown hair. Though she was quite sure she'd never
manage all that stuff floating around her shoulders. She much
preferred the chignon that held the whole mess off her face.

Cecily largely ignored the tales bandied around in the
George and Dragon on a wet and windy night, or whispered
behind a gloved hand while browsing at the white elephant stall
at the church bazaar.

She hired Madeline to do the floral arrangements at the
Pennyfoot Hotel because she was first and foremost a friend,
and because of the woman's knack with flowers, not because
of her reputation for foreseeing the future. So when Madeline
made her announcement, quite naturally Cecily dismissed it as
usual.

"I feel disaster in the air," Madeline said in her low musical
voice that sounded like the wind in the bulrushes on Deep
Willow Pond. "There's a full moon tonight."

Full moons appeared every month, and so far the Pennyfoot
had survived enough of them as well as the wrath of the east
winds for most of the last century and the first six years of this
one. Which was precisely what Cecily told her.

There were more pressing problems to worry about. The
fancy dress ball was scheduled for that night, and there were
still a dozen or more details to be taken care of. And Henry
presented quite a challenge.

Phoebe was in charge of the entertainment at the Pennyfoot's weekly events. Henry was the live python she'd hired to
embellish the tableau she planned to present at the ball.

Cecily had some reservations about Phoebe's ability to

handle an eighteen-foot snake in a crowded ballroom. "There'll be at least sixty guests in attendance tonight," she said, her fingers absently tapping the polished surface of the table. "I shudder to think what would happen if an eighteen-foot snake were to be allowed loose among the dancers on the floor."

At the far end of the table, dwarfed by shelves of dusty volumes that for the most part hadn't been touched in years, Phoebe adjusted the very large brim of her hat. "Mr. Sims assured me that Henry is as docile as a kitten. He's left me full instructions on how to take care of him, and I am quite sure there is nothing to worry about."

Madeline, seated behind a huge bowl of pink and white roses, pursed her lips. "This is not the night to trust a wild animal. All living creatures are unpredictable during a full moon. Lovers quarrel, children run away, husbands cheat, and murderers murder on the night of the full moon."

Phoebe sniffed in disapproval. She tolerated Madeline because of her association with the Pennyfoot but secretly considered her decidedly strange and rather beneath her consideration.

Although Phoebe's clothes had seen better days, they were of good quality, and she had taken very good care of them. In Phoebe's eyes, one's dress indicated character and class, and Madeline's deplorable frocks appeared to denote a definite lack of both.

"I should think that with all my experience," Phoebe said stiffly, "I can be trusted to know what I'm doing." Her face looked small and pinched under her hat. The brim resembled the size of a tea tray and looked just as cumbersome, loaded down as it was with enormous silk gardenias, feathers, and, for good measure, a pair of emaciated doves.

Cecily often wondered how Phoebe's neck, which was long and slender, managed to hold up the weight of such a monstrosity. "I have absolute faith in you, Phoebe," she said, hoping that this meeting wouldn't develop into a battle of wits between the two women.

Her gaze fell on the bouquet, arranged by Madeline in a Waterford crystal bowl. The air hung heavy with its fragrance. She noticed a single pink, velvet-soft petal lying forlornly, mirrored in the gleaming surface of the table. Staring at it Cecily was reminded of evening strolls in the gardens with James, enjoying the refreshing breezes saturated with the sweet perfume of roses.

She glanced up at the portrait that hung over the marble fireplace. Her late husband had looked so handsome in his military uniform. Even now, six months later, she found it so difficult to believe he was gone.

She had recently passed out of full mourning and now favored soft pastel blouses trimmed with black ribbons with her black skirts. Although her appearance might have lightened, her heart still ached for her loss.

Who would have thought that the malaria he'd contracted in the tropics, ending a brilliant career, would return to take him from her much too soon?

She closed her mind on the thought and concentrated on the task at hand. "Madeline, how are the floral arrangements coming along? Did you manage to find the tiger lilies?"

Apparently absorbed in her own thoughts, Madeline blinked. "Yes, I had them sent down from Covent Garden this morning. I decided on tiger lilies, ginger blossoms, and birds of paradise. A perfect choice, I think, for the Arabian Nights theme. Though I might have a problem with the ferns. They do tend to dry out."

"Ferns in Arabia?" Phoebe took a large pin out of her hat, straightened the brim, and jabbed the pin back in again. The doves bobbed precariously on their perch.

Madeline's dark eyes rested intently on Phoebe's face. "We're not in Arabia. And I always use ferns."

"Ferns will be fine," Cecily said firmly. She closed her ledger with a loud snap to indicate the end of the meeting.

Following Phoebe out, Madeline paused in the doorway. "It has a ring around it," she said.

Cecily stared at her, wondering what her friend meant.

"The moon," Madeline explained, drawing circles in the air with a languid hand. "It has a ring around it. You know what that means."

"It usually means there's another storm brewing in the Channel."

"It means," Madeline murmured, ignoring Cecily's dry comment, "a death." She followed her dramatic pause with a long, drawn-out sigh.

"I'll bear it in mind," Cecily promised, trying not to think about Henry.

Later that day Cecily discovered the loose bricks. The guests, happily established in the dining room, enjoyed a feast of deviled kidneys, cold roast pheasant, and galantines garnished with melon.

Cecily, having already eaten, had gone up to the roof garden shortly after noon to spend a few moments alone with her thoughts, as was her custom. She and James had spent many an enjoyable respite in this tiny retreat, and she felt close to him whenever she visited the quiet spot.

The wall blocked off the narrow passage between the roofs, and the flat rectangle area had been turned into a small rooftop garden. The slope of the roofs bordered both sides and one short end, while the other finished at the edge of the roof, hence the protection of the wall.

This had become a favorite place for hotel guests to view the stone thatched cottages dotting Parson's Hill or the fishing boats bobbing in the cove. In order to see the entire panorama, one had to lean over the wall. It took only a cursory inspection of the loosened bricks for Cecily to recognize the wall presented a clear danger.

An average person's weight could conceivably collapse part of the wall and send an unsuspecting guest toppling four stories down to the red-brick courtyard below.

Harry Davis, the brick mason, would need a day or two to repair it. Meanwhile, Cecily decided, she needed to do something at once.

The staff would be busy with the lunchtime chores. Since she couldn't shake the sense of urgency over the situation, she fashioned a crude sign from an orange crate and carried it up four flights of stairs to the roof garden.

The rain barrel was half-full of water and resisted her efforts to drag it closer to the wall to support the sign. Struggling to move it, she didn't hear the footsteps behind her. She started violently when a deep voice inquired, "Pray, what are you doing, madam?"

Without turning her head, she muttered, "I should think it's fairly obvious what I'm doing, Baxter. I'm attempting to move this barrel close to the wall."

"Yes, madam. I can see that. To be more precise, I meant *why* are you doing that?"

"I need a support for this sign."

"That is something a footman should be doing. Surely Ian could have done that for you?"

"He could," Cecily agreed, grunting with exertion. "I didn't ask him, however. He has his own duties to be concerned about."

She hadn't noticed that she stood on the hem of her long skirt until she tried to straighten her back. Momentarily set off balance, she grabbed the edge of the barrel. "Trousers, Baxter. That's what I need, trousers. Like those knickerbockers women wear nowadays for riding bicycles."

"I hardly think so, madam." He stepped forward and took hold of the barrel. "Allow me?"

She eyed her manager's impressive build in the immaculate black morning coat and crisp white shirt. "You'll get dirty, Baxter."

"I'll take care, madam."

She clung to it for a moment, reluctant to give up. "Perhaps if we both push?"

"I would rather manage on my own."

"Oh, very well." She stepped back, her frustration increasing when she saw how easily he maneuvered the heavy barrel into position. She reached for the signpost, but he stopped her with a disapproving gleam in his eyes.

"Oh, come now, Baxter. You are not going to throw that 'helpless little woman' attitude at me, are you? You surely know better."

"I happen to believe, madam, that there are some tasks that could be more appropriately assigned to the staff."

"And if I waited for someone to do half of them, they would never get done. Besides, if you read the sign, I'm sure you'll agree with me that some urgency was warranted."

Baxter tilted back on the heels of his immaculately polished shoes and examined the heavily scrawled letters. "Danger! Keep off!" he read out loud, sounding as if he were announcing a rather distasteful breakfast menu. "Wall under repair. Extremely dangerous."

She watched his face for his reaction and, as usual, could detect none. "Well? So what do you think?"

"It certainly draws attention to the problem." He glanced at the wall, which served as a barrier at the edge of the roof. "A dire message indeed."

"And necessary," Cecily said firmly. "There are several loose bricks in that one spot. I can't imagine how the wall could get in that state without someone noticing it before. Must have been all those fierce winds we've had lately. I've sent a message to the mason to take care of it as soon as possible, but I don't want anyone to go near the wall until it's been repaired." She shuddered. "If someone should lean against it to admire the view . . ."

"I understand perfectly." Baxter wedged the sign between the barrel and the wall. "But I would feel far more comfortable if you would not take it upon yourself to perform the manual labor."

She knew she should ignore the remark. But something inside her prodded her into saying, "I traveled half the world with my husband, Baxter, rearing two sons, occasionally in conditions that would horrify the hardiest of men. I hardly think this compares, do you?"

She could see the glint of displeasure in his eyes. Baxter had the kind of light gray eyes that could freeze the icing on a hot cross bun.

"It is not your place, madam."

"But it is my hotel."

"And as owner of this establishment, you should observe a certain level of decorum."

"Piffle!"

She saw his jaw tense but he refrained from answering. Feeling remorse for offending him, she softened her tone. "Baxter, I appreciate your concern, you know that. And I'm not trying to interfere with your duties. But I am used to running a household and a family. Now that the house is sold and I am living here in the hotel, I find myself with too much time on my hands. Too much time to think.''

She paused to control the quiver of pain she always felt at the thought of her dead husband. ''And I am perfectly capable of manual labor. I might be past forty, but I still have my health and strength.''

''I apologize, madam. It's none of my business. I didn't mean to infer—''

''It's all right, Baxter.'' She summoned a smile. ''Was there a particular reason you followed me up here?''

''Yes, madam.'' He hesitated, as if reluctant to tell her more.

Wondering what new problem awaited her, she braced herself for bad news.

CHAPTER

✿2✿

Baxter stared out at the shimmering coastline, looking uncomfortable. "It's Gertie. I'm afraid she's in a spot of bother. I thought that you should be made aware of what's happened."

Cecily shook her head in despair. The housemaid was a diligent employee, but constantly in hot water. "Who has she upset now?"

"It appears that Lady Eleanor Danbury has mislaid a brooch. She has accused Gertie of stealing it and is insisting on sending for the constable."

"Oh, Lord. Have you talked to Gertie?"

"Gertie swears she didn't take the brooch. When I left her in the kitchen, she was extremely upset."

"I can imagine. What about Lady Eleanor?"

"I have not discussed it with her yet. I thought of asking Mrs. Chubb to have a word with her, but I doubt that milady would condescend to speak with the housekeeper."

With a hint of mischief, Cecily murmured, "Why, Baxter, are you suggesting I should confront the dragon in its lair?"

He ran a finger under his stiff, white collar. "I just thought that milady might be more inclined to listen to someone of your standing."

She uttered a short laugh at that. "If Lady Eleanor had the slightest inkling of my financial woes, she would no doubt brush me off as if I were nothing more than a tiresome gnat. But I daresay she'll agree to receive me, so I'll pay her a visit later."

Baxter looked vastly relieved. "Thank you, madam."

"I'm sure the situation will turn out to be a simple misunderstanding. Gertie might have her problems, but I simply can't imagine her stealing. I'll have a word with her, too."

"It's her afternoon off. She won't return until half past six."

"Very well, it will have to be then." Cecily reached out and touched a silky rose petal. "Lady Eleanor can be so difficult. James was always so good at smoothing out these little problems."

"Yes, madam."

Her smile felt a little bleak. "Thank you for your help, Baxter."

He looked at her for a moment longer, then said quietly, "I miss him, too, madam." He dipped his head and turned smartly on his heel to head for the narrow door to the stairway.

Her smile fading, Cecily took a last look around. The fragrance of roses, a mass of dark red blooms planted in the huge wooden tubs, mingled with the scent of honeysuckle, carefully trained to climb the trellis on each side of the garden.

From where she stood she could see beyond the Point to the lighthouse on one side and the gentle slope of cliffs that formed the curve on the other.

The windows of the shops along the Esplanade sparkled in the reflection from the water, and a nanny slowly pushed a baby in a perambulator close by the railings, the ribbons of her white cap streaming behind her.

Beyond the pair, the morning mist had thinned to a haze across the shining ripples of the ocean, and sunlight turned the sand to silver. The panorama looked serene for the moment, though the thick band of gray at the horizon posed the threat of a storm later.

Cecily watched a sea gull swoop low across the water, its cry carrying clearly on the summer breeze. At times like these, she thought, it was easy to imagine how peaceful Badgers End must have been before its quaint charms had been discovered by the pleasure-seeking members of London's aristocracy.

A dull buzz in the distance grew to a roar as a red motor car crested the hill and began its tortuous climb down toward the cove. Although the sight of a car was becoming more familiar, it still seemed out of place, a symbol of the new world invading the old.

Cecily watched the noisy vehicle until it disappeared from view, then after a last, concerned glance at the damaged wall, she turned to follow Baxter through the doorway.

Cecily had to wait until late afternoon before Lady Eleanor would receive her. Milady was taking a nap, her paid companion, Daphne Morris, informed Cecily.

Miss Morris was also tall, but had the kind of frail bone structure for which Cecily would gladly have traded once upon a time. Happily she was long past such wishful thinking, or so she told herself as she exchanged pleasantries with milady's companion.

Daphne Morris had a much coveted position in an affluent household. As a lady's companion, she enjoyed many privileges, traveling with milady wherever she went, staying in establishments the like of which she could never have afforded otherwise.

The companion was responsible for milady's wardrobe, her hair, and her general comfort. In exchange, she had her own quarters in the family section of the house, a generous salary, and more than adequate free time to pursue her own interests.

It would seem an enviable vocation to many, though Cecily was quite certain that had she not had the good fortune to marry James at an early age, a position as a lady's companion would have been the last resort.

The idea of dancing attendance night and day on a petulant,

bored aristocrat whose main goal in life was to outshine her acquaintances in fripperies and finery was not Cecily's cup of tea at all. In fact, she had no doubt that in very short order she would have been dismissed for insubordination.

Which is why she felt a certain sympathy toward Gertie and her never-ending disputes with the upper crust. Unfortunately Baxter was not as charitable, and had it not been for Cecily's tactful intervention, the belligerent housemaid would have been let go on more than one occasion.

Deciding that it couldn't hurt to have another champion in her corner, Cecily invited Miss Morris up to her suite on the second floor for afternoon tea.

If the companion was surprised by this unexpected honor, she showed no sign of it when she readily agreed.

The Pennyfoot had once been the country home of the Earl of Saltchester, until ten years earlier, when the family fortune had been lost and they were forced to sell.

The seaside holiday was just beginning to come into vogue, and James Sinclair, retired from the army, had envisioned a comfortable, respectable establishment for his investment. He intended to provide a holiday resort for the more affluent families who could afford to escape the summer heat of the city.

It hadn't quite turned out that way. Discovered by Society, word spread quickly, and the secluded Pennyfoot had soon become a favorite weekend retreat of the upper class.

Quick to realize the potential, James had refurbished the hotel accordingly, running up huge debts to do so, and raised the rates. Assured of privacy and a guarantee of a discreet staff, the patrons had been happy to pay for the privileges.

There were six suites on the third floor of the Pennyfoot Hotel, one in each corner of the building and one on either side of the stairway.

Cecily occupied the only suite on the second floor. The remainder of the rooms on that floor were sumptuous, but not as spacious as the suites, though they offered more privacy and were in great demand.

The rooms on the first floor were usually occupied by the

less influential visitors, such as Daphne Morris. There were
thirty-five guest rooms in all.

The staff, those of whom lived at the hotel, occupied rooms
below stairs at the basement level, together with the kitchens
and laundries. Above them, the ground floor consisted of the
ballroom cum dining room, library, main lounge, and bar.
Beneath them lay the cellars.

Cecily had become accustomed to her suite, though she still
missed the privacy and freedom of the house she and James
had shared until his death.

Daphne Morris seemed suitably impressed when Cecily
invited her in. She sat on the edge of an elegant brocade Queen
Anne chair as if she were afraid it would break. Her eyes
wandered around the spacious sitting room with a shrewd
expression that made Cecily wonder if she were calculating the
value of everything she saw.

"That is a magnificent elephant tusk," Miss Morris com-
mented.

Cecily glanced up to where the huge ivory horn hung above
the fireplace. "Thank you. It was a gift to my late husband
from an African chief."

Miss Morris shifted uncomfortably on the edge of her chair.
"I—everyone was so very sorry to learn of Major Sinclair's
death. He will be sorely missed by many people."

Cecily nodded, feeling her throat grow tight. "You are most
kind. He will indeed." In an effort to change the subject, she
added, "Tell me, Miss Morris, have you seen many foreign
places during your employment with Lady Eleanor?"

The companion's expression altered slightly, becoming
almost wary. "Yes, indeed I have. It has all been most
interesting."

"I am sure that working for Lady Eleanor must be quite
rewarding."

Cecily could see loyalty struggling with honesty on Miss
Morris's face.

Finally giving Cecily the opening she needed, the younger
woman said quietly, "She is a very fair employer and can be
quite generous at times."

A tap on the door interrupted the conversation, and Cecily

rose to answer it. A housemaid stood in the doorway with a loaded tray. "Your tea, madam," she said, her gaze going past Cecily to stare curiously at the unusual visitor.

"Thank you, Ethel." Cecily stood back to allow the young girl to carry the tray over to the low table in the middle of the room. Setting it down carefully, the maid straightened.

"That will be all, Ethel," Cecily said, smiling.

"Yes, madam." Ethel bobbed her head, then scurried out the door, no doubt anxious to relate the titillating news that Mrs. Sinclair was actually entertaining a paid companion for tea.

Pouring tea from the silver teapot into a bone china cup, Cecily remarked casually, "I'm glad to know that Lady Eleanor is a fair person. I understand there is a problem with one of my maids, something about a lost brooch?"

"Yes, I am afraid so."

Cecily put down the teapot and picked up the small jug of milk. "That is the matter I wish to discuss later with Lady Eleanor." She poured the milk into the cups and put down the jug. Picking up the sugar bowl, she inquired, "One lump or two?"

"One, thank you."

"I hope milady will be reasonable about this," Cecily said, plopping a sugar lump into the cup. "Gertie is a trifle too quick with her tongue at times, but I have known her for five years. I feel certain I can vouch for her honesty."

Daphne Morris accepted the cup and saucer Cecily handed her with murmured thanks. "Well, I don't wish to be indiscreet, but milady has been known to mislay things from time to time."

Cecily picked up a dish laden with triangular cheese and cucumber sandwiches, the crusts neatly sliced from the bread. Another dish held egg and cress sandwiches, and she picked up that one, too, offering both to Miss Morris.

"That is what I thought might be the case," she said. "Perhaps you would be so kind as to hunt for the brooch, just in case it has been dropped somewhere?"

The other woman took one sandwich from each dish and put them on the small plate Cecily had placed with a serviette on the table in front of her. "I will be happy to, though I should mention that I have already searched quite thoroughly."

"I'm quite sure you have. But I would consider it a personal favor if you would do so again. I would be most unhappy if Gertie were to be accused of such a serious offense without justification."

Miss Morris promised to do what she could, and Cecily had to be content with that for the time being. She did her best to make the rest of the younger woman's visit enjoyable, but Daphne Morris seemed ill at ease and kept glancing at the clock on the mantelpiece.

Realizing that she was most likely worried about milady waking from her nap, Cecily felt a twinge of remorse for causing the companion such anxiety, and hoped that the poor woman would not be chastised for her pains.

A member of the Pennyfoot staff had been threatened, however. She had only done her duty. She was quite relieved when she could bring the visit to an end.

Phoebe Carter-Holmes loved her job at the Pennyfoot. Being the local vicar's mother, she was constantly on call for various charities and good deeds, most of which she obliged with good grace. But the Pennyfoot actually paid her for her services, and although some would look upon it as demeaning for a woman of her background, Phoebe certainly wasn't too proud to take what she felt was her due.

Not that she was treated like an employee. Oh, no, that would never do. For one thing, when dear Sedgely was alive and she was still a legitimate member of the Carter-Holmes family, she had twice visited the Pennyfoot when it was still Saltchester Manor. She had very fond memories of the place.

Besides, she and Cecily were friends, and Phoebe accommodated her just to help out. The job took up no more than a couple of days a week and involved a great deal of what she did best—organizing.

Phoebe chose the themes, the orchestra, and the entertainment for each weekly extravaganza at the Pennyfoot. The python was one of her more ambitious ideas, hired at great expense to form the centerpiece of the Arabian Nights tableau at midnight.

She could hardly contain her excitement at the prospect that evening. The masterpiece promised to be her best effort yet, and already she was savoring the accolades from the delighted audience.

She had installed the python, coiled in his basket, in a corner of the laundry room until his debut. The laundry room was an annex to the main building and faced the yard that had been dug out next to the kitchens at the back of the hotel. It made an ideal place to store the various props that Phoebe used in creating her spectacular presentations.

Although it was still an hour or two before the start of the ball, Phoebe couldn't resist peeking in on Henry just to make sure he was comfortable. After all, as Mr. Sims, Henry's quaint little owner had told her, a comfortable snake was a happy snake. And it made perfect sense to Phoebe that a happy snake was not likely to strike out at anyone.

In spite of Mr. Sims's assurance that Henry was docile, she was still a little apprehensive and intended to make sure that Henry was positively delirious with all the attention bestowed upon him.

Holding up the hem of her mauve silk frock to avoid the puddles left from the midweek storm, she bustled across the yard to the laundry room. Several feet from the building she pulled up short.

She had locked the door when she'd left an hour earlier, since the maids would not need clean laundry until the morning. Someone must have been there, however. The door now stood ajar.

With a dreadful sinking feeling in her stomach, Phoebe clutched her lace-bound throat and crept closer. Holding her breath, she peered in.

The lid of Henry's basket lay several feet away, as if someone had flung it aside. The basket, with its red satin cushion still bearing the indentation of the snake, was quite empty. Henry had disappeared.

CHAPTER

3

"I really don't know why you defend the wretched child. It's obvious that she stole the brooch." Lady Eleanor peered into the dressing-table mirror and patted her luxuriant brown hair into place.

"It's possible you could have mislaid the brooch somewhere, milady."

"We have already discussed this, Daphne. You yourself searched for the brooch, did you not?"

"Yes, milady. But—"

"Really, Daphne, I fail to see why you are persisting in this argument." Eleanor glanced at the reflection of her companion in the mirror.

Daphne Morris stood near the fireplace, framed by the maroon-and-white-flocked wallpaper behind her. The white frock she wore accentuated her tall frame, giving her almost an air of elegance. She was ten years Eleanor's junior and quietly attractive, in spite of her large mouth and rather pointed nose.

Eleanor looked back at her own perfect features. The salmon-pink tea gown she wore had cost a small fortune. She'd found it in the Rue de la Paix in Paris that spring, together with that exquisite Worth gown that she'd worn to the Palace ball. The cream silk satin embroidered with golden butterflies had done wonders for her bared shoulders.

Eleanor leaned forward for a closer look. Even so, she'd take Daphne's nose and the big mouth just to have those ten years back. Fast approaching forty, she was only too aware that her looks were beginning to show signs of dreaded old age.

"If the clasp was insecure, the brooch could have fallen anywhere without you noticing it," Daphne said stubbornly.

Eleanor's irritation intensified, and she turned, scowling at her companion. "There was nothing wrong with the clasp. I tell you, that little gutter urchin stole it."

"You can't be certain of that." Daphne seemed determined to stand her ground, furthering Eleanor's annoyance. "To accuse an innocent person without proof is a terrible thing. It could ruin her entire life."

"And you forget your place, Daphne. It is not up to you to tell me whether I am right or wrong. I suggest you keep your opinions to yourself if you want to remain in my employ."

To Eleanor's satisfaction, Daphne pinched her lips together. The threat worked like a charm every time. The woman knew full well it would be near impossible for her to find such lucrative employment elsewhere. At her age and without references, her choices would be limited. That's what kept Daphne in line, plus the fact that she was well paid for her services.

"Isn't it time you took Chan Ying for his walk? The poor little thing is getting restless." Eleanor crouched to scoop up the Pekingese at her slippered feet. "It's those hotel cats. Nasty, vicious things. Always spitting and scratching at him. Upsets his sensitive nature, doesn't it, my little poochy-woochy?"

She buried her face in the soft fur, while the ungrateful little beast wriggled frantically in her arms. No matter what she did, she couldn't seem to associate with this dog. Not like Caesar, poor thing. Sad day when they buried him. He simply adored her. Followed her everywhere.

"I thought I'd go down and collect the costumes for the ball first, milady," Daphne said, reaching for her shawl. "By the time I get back with Chan Ying, it will be time to dress your hair."

"Very well. But please hurry. A storm is brewing out there." Eleanor dropped the Pekingese onto the carpet. Twitching the lace train of her tea gown behind her, she spun around and headed for the window. "I'd hate for the little darling to get wet and catch cold."

"I'll be as quick as I can."

Eleanor pulled back the heavy gold damask curtain and looked out at the heaving sea. The deserted, windswept Esplanade looked quite dismal now that the sun had disappeared. "Look at that," she exclaimed, expecting Daphne to do no such thing. "White horses. And the sky as black as coal. There's always something so ominous about a threatening storm."

"Yes, milady. I'll leave right now."

Eleanor turned as the door opened. Robert hurried in, narrowly avoiding a collision with Daphne on her way out. She ducked her head and scurried past him as if she expected a scolding.

Eleanor had no idea why her husband should intimidate the woman that way. Daphne had no such problem when contradicting her employer. But then she seemed to have a problem where all men were concerned. That's what came of being a spinster, no doubt.

She waited until Daphne had closed the door behind her before eyeing Robert's handsome features with suspicion. "Where have you been all afternoon? Gambling, I suppose. You absolutely reek of cigar smoke."

"Now, now, my precious, you know I don't waste my money on such sinful recreation." Smiling sheepishly, Robert advanced toward her.

Avoiding his outstretched hand, she moved over to a peacock-blue brocade sofa. "My money, you mean. Don't think I don't know where you sneak off to while I'm napping.

You men are all alike. I saw your friend Keith today. Utterly disgusting, that's all I can say for him.''

Robert looked surprised. "Keith? Here in the Pennyfoot? I wasn't aware he was coming down here.''

Eleanor uttered a brittle laugh. "Neither was Luella, I wager. Little does she know the man to whom she's betrothed and about to marry is dallying in a seaside hotel with a fallen woman.'' She'd delivered the last two words with great relish, enjoying the startled look on her husband's face.

"You saw her—this woman?''

Smoothing out her skirt, Eleanor lowered herself gracefully onto the sofa. "No, of course not. He had her hidden somewhere, of course. Most likely in that ghastly motor car of his.''

Draping her arm along the back of the sofa, she gave him a smug smile. "But I saw him signing in. I waited until he left, then went up to ask that dim-witted fool at the desk about the theme for tonight's fancy dress ball. He never even noticed me staring at the guest register, he was too busy fawning over me. Silly man.''

"And you love it,'' Robert murmured.

Eleanor narrowed her eyes. "What does that mean?''

"Nothing my precious, nothing at all.'' Robert sank down next to her and took hold of her hand. "Why wouldn't any number of men covet my beautiful, desirable wife? How they must envy my good fortune, my dearest.'' He lifted her hand and pressed his lips to her fingers.

Eleanor withdrew her hand and stood up. "Don't you want to know what I saw in the register?''

"Tell me what you saw, my sweet.''

"Keith actually had the nerve to sign the register as Mr. and Mrs. Torrington. Can you believe that? I can hardly wait to get back to town and inform Luella what a dreadful cad she's planning to wed.''

Robert rose smartly from the sofa. "Now wait a minute, my precious. You're not going to tell Luella about this, are you? I mean, the wedding is all set for next month. It will be the biggest society bash in months. Everyone who is anyone will be there.''

Eleanor bared her teeth in a triumphant grin. "If there *is* a wedding. I imagine once Luella gets wind of this, she will send Mr. Keith Torrington packing. And good riddance, I say!"

"But, my dear—"

Eleanor held up her hand. "Not another word, Robert. I will not change my mind about this. It's my duty to warn my very best friend before she makes an utter fool of herself." She stepped back, starting as a loud squeal erupted behind her.

"Oh, Channy, precious, I'm so sorry." She picked up the Pekingese and stroked his back. "Incidentally, Robert, I'm afraid I have more bad news. One of the maids has stolen my emerald brooch. The one with the diamonds around it? I know I left it right there on the dresser, and now it's gone."

With a look of anxiety creasing his brow, Robert crossed the room to the dresser. "Are you sure, my dearest? You haven't simply misplaced it?"

"Of course I'm sure. I had a word with the girl. Guilt was written all over her face. You know how well I read people. Besides, she was the only one in this room, except for Daphne, and that one would never steal from me. She doesn't have the gumption for one thing, and she well knows on what side her bread is buttered."

She frowned at Robert, who stood aimlessly moving objects around on the dresser. "It's no good looking for it, Robert. Daphne and I searched this room from top to bottom. It's gone, I tell you, and I know where it's gone. Stolen by that wretched little servant. I told her I was reporting it to the constable at the very first opportunity."

"If you must, my sweet. And while you're about it, perhaps you would mention my letter opener to him? It seems to have disappeared as well."

Eleanor gasped. "Not the pretty silver one? But, darling, the jewels in that handle are priceless. Perhaps we should go through everything. Heaven knows what that nasty little thief might have taken." She hurried over to the dresser. "What on earth is the Pennyfoot coming to, hiring such riffraff? It never used to be like this when James was alive. Just goes to prove that women have no business trying to do men's work." Furiously she began sorting through her jewelry.

*   *   *

Phoebe stared at the empty basket, willing herself not to faint. It couldn't be. Surely not. Henry was eighteen feet long. How could he have slithered across the yard without someone seeing him? Who had left the door open? Most important of all, where was Henry now?

She felt a cold wave of panic sweep over her, and she swayed to and fro. No, she couldn't faint. She had to find Henry before he found someone to feed on. Great merciful heavens, what was she going to do?

Turning, Phoebe grabbed hold of the doorjamb to steady herself. She should tell someone. She couldn't do this all alone. Cecily. No, Cecily would kill her. Mr. Baxter? No. She was terrified of Mr. Baxter. Besides, he'd insist on telling Cecily. Oh, God, Cecily would never trust her again.

She began trotting across the yard, looking left and right, not really knowing where she was going. To make matters worse, a drop of rain plopped on her nose. Her best silk gown would be ruined, not to mention her hat. But that was the least of her worries for now.

What if Henry actually ate someone? Would Phoebe be arrested? How would that look? The vicar's mother, in prison for allowing a dangerous animal to escape. Oh, good Lord, she had to find that snake. And she needed help. Urgently.

She needed to go to the lavatory. She didn't have time to go to the lavatory. She'd have to hold it. She just hoped the rain would hold off.

She reached the rose garden and let out a sigh of relief. There, crouched under a bright yellow rosebush, knelt the one man who could help her, the one man she could trust to keep her secret.

With one whisper that a full-sized python was on the loose in the hotel grounds, pandemonium was assured. She had to find the dratted thing before anyone discovered her mishap.

A low growl of thunder prodded her into action. She hurried forward, calling out the groundskeeper's name in an urgent, fierce whisper. "John. *John!* You have to help me. Oh, please, you must help me."

He lifted his head as she approached, regarding her with an

expression of wary dismay. John Thimble tended to be reticent around people. He'd spent the better part of his sixty years avoiding women entirely.

"John!" Phoebe gasped, clutching the sleeve of his shirt, "I really don't know what I'm going to do. Oh, my. This is so bad for my heart. I hope I don't faint."

John jumped to his feet so fast he nearly lost his balance. His look of alarm suggested he, too, passionately hoped she wouldn't faint.

Phoebe summoned her strength and held out pleading hands. "You simply must help me find him. I have no one else I can turn to."

He focused his eyes in the region of her large, flower-bedecked hat. "Now hold on, missus, hold on. What be the trouble, then?"

"It's Henry. He's escaped!" The last word came out as a shriek, and Phoebe made a desperate attempt to calm herself. "We must find him. Heaven knows what he'll do if someone treads on him. Mr. Sims assured me he was sluggish, but I mean, how docile can you expect him to be with a foot on his stomach?"

John blinked. "Henry? I don't think I be acquainted with him, missus."

Phoebe tilted her upper body forward and peered up at him from beneath the wide brim of her hat. "Henry is a snake," she hissed. "A very big snake."

That got his attention. "A snake?"

"Yes." For heaven's sake, did he have to repeat everything? "If we don't find him right away, he could bite someone."

"What kind of snake be it, then?"

Phoebe felt quite sure she was going to scream. What difference did it make, for pity's sake? "Henry's a python." She spread her arms out at her sides as far as they would reach. "His head is this big."

John pulled off his cap and scratched his thick white hair. "I reckon he won't bite, missus. Pythons are more partial to squeezing, so's I've heard."

With a howl of frustration, Phoebe grabbed John's arm.

"They eat goats, John. Goats! He's out here somewhere in the gardens—"

John's lined and weathered face registered real concern, and his gaze finally bumped into hers. "The gardens? Why didn't you say so before, then? Come, we best find him right away before he do some damage."

They started their search in the rose gardens, peering and prodding under every bush. At least, John did the prodding. Phoebe kept well back in case Henry should take offense at a poke from the garden rake. A sleeping snake presented a very different threat than a cornered python on the rampage.

Henry was not in the rose garden, nor was he lying in the rock pool. Neither the croquet lawn nor the grass tennis court revealed any sign of the python's huge body, and Phoebe felt genuinely light-headed with all the anxiety.

When John suggested the courtyard with its sun-warmed bricks, her hopes rose. Just the place for a snake to seek refuge, though the rain pattering down could have disturbed Henry's sanctuary by now.

Thick laurel hedges, eight feet tall, bordered the courtyard on all four sides. The narrow entrance barely gave one person passage, and Phoebe allowed John to pass through before shuffling her sodden shoes anxiously behind him. Once inside, she waited as John began poking under the hedge.

Already the storm had darkened the evening, bringing an early dusk. At first Phoebe thought the wind had scattered pieces of laurel about. Then lightning danced across the dark red surface of the ground, and she saw that the laurel was in fact chunks of brick. In the same instant, the white-hot light bathed a bundle of wet clothes lying on the rockery in the corner. A second later it vanished, so suddenly Phoebe thought she'd imagined it.

She heard John's grunt of surprise, and her stomach seemed to drop like a bucket down a well. Even without the lightning, she could now see a pair of satin shoes sticking out from the wet bundle. Dancing shoes. And they still clung to a pair of feet.

Thunder rumbled closer, longer, then erupted with an angry bellow. Phoebe shrieked, her hand slapping her mouth as if to stop the sound. From the open French windows of the ballroom came the lilting strains of the opening waltz. The ball had begun, minus one of its guests.

Unable to move, Phoebe watched John creep closer, his slight stoop hunching his broad shoulders. He knelt by the side of the macabre mound and reached out a hand.

Shivering, Phoebe waited for the worst. How was she going to tell dear Algie his mother was responsible for a death by python? She felt sick. And she desperately needed to go to the lavatory.

Slowly John turned his head to look at her. Just at that moment another blinding flash transformed his face into a white blob. "From the looks of the bloody mess her head be in," he observed quietly, "it be very likely the lady be dead."

Phoebe's legs gave way, and she sat down hard on the drenched bricks. It didn't seem to matter, anyway, since she'd already wet her drawers. Her lips seemed to be imprisoned in ice. "Who . . . who is it?"

John's voice seemed very loud in the hush that followed the thunder. "It be Lady Eleanor Danbury, Mum."

CHAPTER

❈ 4 ❈

Cecily had enjoyed one saving grace when competing with her brothers—her height. By the time she was fifteen she equaled her youngest brother's stature of five feet six. At eighteen she'd come close to her eldest brother at five feet nine.

There weren't too many women who looked her straight in the eye, but Gertie Brown was one of them. When it came to width, however, Gertie easily exceeded her. Built like the conventional farmer's daughter, the housemaid actually hailed from London. In a reversal of tradition, at twelve years old she'd sought a position in a seaside town to escape what she called "the 'orrible muck and racket."

James Sinclair had hired her for her strength and her forthright manner, the latter of which he'd regretted on more than one occasion.

Cecily, for the most part, found Gertie's enthusiasm refreshing, but at that moment the girl's usually pale face glowered with temper. She stood with her back to the gleaming black fireplace in the tiny sitting room, her fists dug into her fleshy hips that no corset could diminish.

Altheda Chubb, head housekeeper of the Pennyfoot, hovered anxiously close by, doing her best to look unobtrusive. It was difficult to do in such cramped quarters.

From the kitchens across the hall wafted the delectable aromas from a dozen mouth-watering dishes that had been carried to the ballroom minutes before. Cecily realized she was hungry. It was already eight o'clock, and she hadn't yet eaten. She'd spent the last half hour looking for Gertie.

"I didn't take the blinking brooch, and Miss Hoity Toity blinking knows it," Gertie declared. "Where does she come orf accusing me of thieving?"

"Just tell me what happened," Cecily said, "and do try not to fabricate."

Gertie looked hurt. "What, me? Never!"

Mrs. Chubb folded plump arms across her bountiful breasts and grunted a warning. Although a good deal shorter than Gertie, the housekeeper matched her in girth and temper. Mrs. Chubb's position forbade her to interrupt her employer, but nevertheless she managed to convey her own authority.

Gertie scowled and stared down at her shoes peeking out from under the hem of her dark blue skirt. Cecily noticed the housemaid's white cap had slid to one side, but decided that could wait for the moment. "Go on, Gertie."

"All right. But I am telling the truth now, Mrs. Sinclair, honest. I didn't take no brooch. I went up there 'coz Mr. Danbury told me his ink bottle was empty. So I took some up there and filled it, and just as I was leaving, in comes that—"

She broke off, slid a sideways glance at Mrs. Chubb, and finished quietly. "Lady Eleanor Danbury, with her lady's companion."

"Mr. Danbury wasn't there?"

"No, mum, he wasn't. I mean, I didn't see him, anyhow."

"So what happened then?"

"Well, milady asked me what I was doing there, and I said as how I was filling the ink bottle and I shows her the ink jar in me hand. Well, she goes straight across to her dresser, don't she, and lo and behold announces that her bleeding—''

Mrs. Chubb clicked her tongue against the roof her mouth. Cecily gave her a slight shake of her head. Gertie's swearing had become a natural part of her speech pattern, and Cecily had long ago given up on weaning the girl from the habit.

''—brooch were missing,'' Gertie finished, without breaking stride. ''I tells her, polite-like, as how I never touched it, but she's screaming and yelling that she's sending for the bobby. Tells me to get out, she does. Then Miss Morris, she puts a word in, says as how milady might have dropped it, but that moo wasn't having none of it. Made up her mind, she 'ad.''

Out of the corner of her eye Cecily could see Mrs. Chubb's bosom bristling with outrage at Gertie's insolence. One of the hotel cats, there to keep down the mice, slunk past the irate housekeeper, who aimed a kick at it with her foot.

Cecily felt sorry for Gertie. The poor child would very likely bear the brunt of the housekeeper's sharp tongue the minute Cecily was out of sight. As if the housemaid didn't have enough to worry about.

Apparently unconcerned, Gertie plowed on. ''That Miss Morris is a bit of all right, she is. Usually them lady's companions are so blooming toffee-nosed they wouldn't see a pile of cow shit till they'd stepped in it. Think they're better than the likes of us, they do. Load of bloody cod's wallop, that's what I says.''

Mrs. Chubb made a desperate sound in the back of her throat.

Taking pity on the housekeeper, Cecily nodded her head. ''Very well, I'll see what I can do. Perhaps by now they've found the brooch. Try not to worry, Gertie. I'm quite sure we can get this matter taken care of without any undue unpleasantness.''

Cecily left quickly, Mrs. Chubb's harsh voice already echoing around the kitchen as the door swung to behind her. Poor Gertie was in hot water this time.

Reaching the foyer, Cecily saw Colonel Fortescue, looking flamboyant as usual in his regimental dress uniform, making straight for her. It was too late to pretend she hadn't seen him. She arranged a smile on her face and prayed someone would rescue her before she had to be rude.

Out of the corner of her eye she saw Robert Danbury heading for the stairs, but he was too far away and in too much of a hurry to pretend a need to speak to him.

The colonel's ruddy face bore a worried frown as he bore down on her. Sir Frederick Fortescue had fought in the Boer War, narrowly escaping death when a shell exploded within feet of him. The shock had left him with a slight stutter, a rapid and constant blinking of his watery, bloodshot eyes, and, according to some less benevolent folk, permanent damage to his brain.

"So glad I caught you, Mrs. Sinclair. Haven't seen my pith helmet anywhere, have you? Put it down for just a minute and now I can't find the pesky thing. Dashed nuisance, that."

"Where did you leave it, Colonel?"

"Hung it on the umbrella stand, old girl, over there by the front door. Only for a minute while I went to get a quick snifter. When I came back, by Jove, it had gone."

He leaned closer, breathing gin fumes in Cecily's face. "Don't want to think someone stole it, old bean. Nasty bit of work, that."

Guessing that the befuddled man had most likely left the helmet in his room, Cecily said soothingly, "Oh, I'm sure no one in this hotel would do such a dreadful thing. It's very likely somewhere around. I'll have my manager look for it for you."

The colonel beamed. "You will? Dashed decent of you, old girl. Went all through the war with that thing, saved my life more than once. Wouldn't want to lose it, you know."

Ten minutes later, Cecily was still trying to put an end to his somewhat exaggerated tales of his army exploits.

"If you'll excuse me, Colonel," she said, feeling a little desperate, "I really must—"

The colonel's luxuriant winter-white mustache twitched with excitement as he leaned forward. Just about intoxicating Cecily with his gin-laced breath, he muttered, "I say, old girl, a little bird told me the theme for tonight's ball is Arabian Nights. Is that right? What? What?"

Cecily's smile remained fixed as she assured him he'd heard correctly.

"I say, what screaming fun. 'Pon my word, should be a ripping time. Yes, indeed." Blinking furiously, he leaned in closer. "Got those dancing girls, have we? Know what I mean, what?"

Cecily grimly held her breath while he drew an hourglass shape in the air with his hands. "Flimsy veils and all that rot, what?" He attempted a wink, but it lost its impact in the midst of his blinking.

"I'm sure you will enjoy the presentation, Colonel. Now if you'll excuse me—"

The front door banged loudly as someone entered the foyer. The colonel shot up in the air. "Great Scott! Here they come! To the battlements, men! Fight to the death!" With a blood-curdling howl, he brandished an imaginary sword and disappeared down the hallway.

Cecily barely saw him go. Her gaze was fixed on the two figures moving slowly toward her. Phoebe appeared to be sleepwalking, her eyes half-closed in a dead-white face. The wide brim of her hat hung limply to her shoulders, dripping water onto her already sodden frock.

But it was the look on John's face that alerted Cecily, a look that spelled a far more serious problem than Phoebe's bedraggled state.

A muffled rumble of thunder filtered through the windows, and for some reason Cecily's mind sped back to Madeline's ominous warning.

"I don't know what's got into you, lately, so help me I don't," Mrs. Chubb declared, having exhausted the list of sins the hapless Gertie had committed. "You know better than to speak that way in front of madam. I couldn't believe my ears. The nerve of it!"

Gertie scuffed the toe of her shoe on the carpet, and the cat pounced for it. The housemaid clamped her mouth shut and refused to look up as Mrs. Chubb went on warming once more to her theme.

"And where have you been for the last half hour? You were

supposed to be here at half past seven. Mrs. Sinclair has been looking for you all over the place.''

"I had to deliver a message," Gertie mumbled.

"A message? Who to?"

"Lady Eleanor."

"And that took you thirty minutes?"

Gertie looked up, her expression defiant. "I bumped into that daffy colonel on the way back. He said as how he'd lost his watch, so I helped him look for it."

"And did you find it?"

"Nah, he had it in his waistcoat pocket all the time, nutty old ponce.''

Mrs. Chubb's hand itched to slap her face. "That's enough, young lady. You know better than to speak about the guests that way. And look at you! You're a disgrace to the Pennyfoot name. Cap on sideways, button missing on your pinafore! Go and fetch the button tin from the larder right now and sew one back on this minute, miss.''

Gertie began stomping toward the larder, which led off Mrs. Chubb's sitting room, but the housekeeper wasn't finished yet. She never used one sentence when three would do more good. It was her job to keep the maids in line, and she was determined that they knew exactly who was in charge.

"And put that cat out. I don't know how it gets in here, I'm sure I don't.''

"Comes in through the larder window from the yard," Gertie mumbled. "I seen it the other morning jumping through there.''

"Well, never mind that now. Just get that button. And be quick about it. The ball's already begun, and they'll be bringing the dirty dishes back any minute. And where's that Ethel? She should have been here by now. Can't rely on no one anymore, I can't. It's all those high falutin' ideas them suffragettes are putting into all you young girls. No good will come of it, you mark my words.''

Gertie emerged from the larder, carrying a square blue biscuit tin. She dumped it on the floor, then squatted down to prise off the lid and began sorting through Mrs. Chubb's colorful collection of buttons. "Ethel said she had a bellyache this morning. P'raps she's lying on her bed."

"Not if she wants her job, she won't be." Her wrath now directed in another direction, Mrs. Chubb could afford to let up on Gertie.

She stalked over to a mahogany rolltop desk in the corner, her keys jangling on the ring at her belt. "Can't let a little thing like that stop us. We all have to put up with the curse. God knows I've had my days when I could've done with a lie down. Just can't give into it, that's all. Grin and bear it, that's what I say. What would the world come to, if we all laid down every time we had a stomachache?"

"I bet the toffs lie down when they get one."

Mrs. Chubb slid up the lid of the desk and opened one of the drawers inside. "Yes, well, we're not the toffs, are we? Don't know as if I'd want to be. Spending all their time trying to work out how to spend their money, all trying to outdo each other with their posh motor cars and their Worth gowns and those ridiculous fancy dress costumes."

She found a spool of white cotton thread and some needles threaded through a folded slip of paper. "Don't know where it's all going to end, I'm sure I don't. Poor old queen Victoria would turn over in her grave, she would, if she could see what her son has done to this country."

Gertie noisily shut the lid back onto the biscuit tin. "Haven't noticed you doing too bleeding bad out of it."

"Here, watch your tongue, you cheeky monkey." Mrs. Chubb pulled out a needle and dropped the rest back in the drawer. "I earn my money the honest way, by working my fingers to the bone for it."

"Yeah, not like the toffs, hey? Some of 'em marry it, like that Robert Danbury for one."

"Yes, well, it's not our place to gossip, I'm sure."

Gertie wasn't about to be sidetracked from her favorite subject. "Well, everyone knows he married that stuck-up bitch for her money. Not that it did her any bleeding good, anyway. What she don't know is he's having a bit on the side. She'd have a cow if she knew that. Serves her bloody well right."

"Gertie, I'll thank you not to use that gutter language in here.

I've told you a thousand times . . .'' She slammed the lid back down on the desk. Valiantly she struggled, but the temptation was too great. ''How do you know?''

Gertie grinned. She picked up the tin and carried it back to the larder, saying with a toss of her head, ''Wouldn't you like to know?''

Mrs. Chubb pinched her lips together. She would dearly like to know, but she wasn't going to let Gertie have that satisfaction. If she waited long enough, the dreadful child wouldn't be able to resist telling her.

Gertie trudged back, her eyes glinting with expectation. She looked disappointed when the housekeeper handed her the needle and cotton.

''Sew that button on now.'' Mrs. Chubb busied herself folding napkins and watched Gertie out of the corner of her eye.

The housemaid bit off a length of the cotton with her teeth, then stuck the end of it between her lips. After a moment she drew it from her mouth, held up the needle, then scrunched up her face and made several ineffective dabs at the eye of the needle with the wet end of the cotton.

Mrs. Chubb stood it as long as she could, then exploded. ''Oh, for heaven's sake, give it to me.'' She took the needle and with one deft movement threaded the cotton through it. ''Here, now sew.''

Gertie took off her pinafore and sat down on the padded coal box at the corner of the fireplace. ''Ethel,'' she said.

Mrs. Chubb frowned. ''What about Ethel?''

''She's the one what told me about Robert Danbury.'' Gertie closed her eyes and tilted her head back. ''Oo, 'andsome devil, he is. I wouldn't mind being done by that one, I can tell you.''

Mrs. Chubb tutted her disapproval, but was too fascinated by now to interrupt with a scolding. ''How does Ethel know?''

Gertie opened her eyes and smiled. ''She saw him. He was coming out of a room on the second floor, while his missus is waiting for him in her room on the floor upstairs.''

Mrs. Chubb swallowed. ''That doesn't mean anything. Mr. Danbury could have been visiting a friend.''

''Yeah, a friend with long blond hair and big tits. A lot

younger than his wife, so Ethel reckons.'' Gertie jabbed the needle into the white cotton fabric and yelped. ''Gawd, strewth! Right through me bloody finger.''

Deciding she'd heard enough, Mrs. Chubb established her authority once more. ''If you don't stop using that filthy language, I'll have to wash your mouth out with soap, young lady.''

''Well, it bloody hurt.'' Gertie stuck the finger in her mouth, sucked on it, then pulled it out with a loud plop. ''Anyway, she got what she bleeding deserves, that's what I say. Nasty, mean-tempered bitch.''

''Gert-*ay*!''

Knowing when she'd gone far enough, Gertie wisely shut up.

The door flew open a few seconds later, and all thoughts of Robert Danbury were wiped out of Mrs. Chubb's mind.

Phoebe stood in the doorway, looking like a drowned scarecrow, with a look on her face as if she'd seen the devil himself.

CHAPTER

✿ 5 ✿

If anyone were to mention Badgers End in the elegant, discreet tea rooms of Edwardian London, more often than not the speaker would be greeted with a blank stare. Badgers End, such as it was, could never be termed a popular seaside resort, like Brighton, for instance.

Badgers End was really little more than a village. As Gertie often remarked, the place was as dull as a wet Sunday afternoon. The biggest excitement came from watching the sea gulls fight over a piece of bread.

Whereon Mrs. Chubb invariably suggested that Gertie find somewhere else to live if all she was interested in was excitement.

Few people would disagree with Gertie. The tiny shops along the Esplanade attracted the ladies, who peered from beneath dainty parasols at the useless knickknacks behind the leaded bay windows. Dolly Matthews ran a quaint little tea shop in the High Street; her chelsea buns and fairy cakes had to be sampled to be believed.

The grassy slopes of Putney Downs provided the perfect updraft from the east wind to send a kite almost up to the clouds, and no one could dispute that the loudest laughter and the wildest tales could be heard in the public bar of the George and Dragon.

The summer visitors to Badgers End were not interested in such pastoral pursuits, however. The tiny village had what all those big, fancy, pleasure-promising resorts didn't have. Badgers End had the Pennyfoot Hotel. Now that was a name the upper crust recognized.

Several days of breathing in the pristine sea air was a guaranteed cure for the respiratory ailments that plagued the citizens of smog-bound cities. In truth, the benefits of the ozone made a handy excuse for the less commendable reasons some of the clients sought the shelter of the Pennyfoot's discreet charm.

Less than seventy miles from London, the secluded hotel offered ample opportunity for bored city dwellers to dally with Lady Luck in the card rooms or taste the forbidden fruits of hanky-panky in the silk and satin boudoirs.

Even so, no hint of scandal ever touched the name of the Pennyfoot. Though the staff might gossip, as indeed they did, no word had ever been leaked outside the hotel walls. Their jobs depended on it. The success of the hotel depended on it.

All that was about to change, Cecily thought, as she followed Baxter and John Thimble into the courtyard. The flickering light from the hurricane lamps illuminated the scene.

Her mind seem to register the tiniest details, as if needing to implant them for posterity. Chunks from the roof garden wall had gouged the surface of the courtyard floor. It would cost a fortune to replace the polished bricks. Most likely the entire area would have to be resurfaced.

Her wet skirt flapped dismally around her ankles as the salty wind scurried in from the sea. The scent of roses mingled with the earthy odor of clean, damp soil, seeming somehow appropriate for the smell of death.

She tilted her head back slowly, reluctant to confirm what

she already knew. Against the darkening sky, the ugly gap in the outline of the wall was a stark accusation of her own negligence.

If only she'd spotted the damage earlier. It could have been repaired by now. A woman's death would not then lie heavy on her conscience, as it surely would for the rest of her days. Madeline's omen had been fulfilled after all.

Thunder rolled in the distance from the dying storm, and she dropped her chin. Some feet from where the men struggled to lift the lifeless body of Lady Eleanor off the jagged rocks, a pitiful pile of uprooted edelweiss tangled with a yellow rock rose.

Cecily saw John take great care to step over the torn plants, as he and Baxter carried the dead woman through the gap in the hedge. With a last guilty glance at the roof, Cecily shook her head and followed the men back to the hotel.

She had argued with Baxter about the wisdom of moving the body before the police constable arrived. But, as she had told her manager, she could not in all good conscience, leave milady out there in the cold, wet night. Even if the poor woman didn't know the difference. And if Baxter suspected that Cecily's concern was more for the possibility of an unsuspecting guest coming upon the body than for the dead woman herself, he'd refrained from saying so.

Rather than risk being seen by a stray guest or two, she directed Baxter to cross the lawn to the library rather than enter through the front door. She then hurried back through the front entrance to unlock the library's French windows.

She watched the men lay their burden down on the polished hardwood floor in front of the bookshelves. The poor woman must have fallen head first to suffer so much damage.

The clothing seemed to make it all the more incongruous. Lady Eleanor had obviously dressed for the ball before going to the roof garden. The Queen Elizabeth costume was a popular choice for the fancy dress balls. This was one queen who would never enjoy the glory.

Blood from her crushed skull had soaked into the tall white ruff she wore around her neck, and the once beautiful satin and brocade dress had been ripped in the fall. Little pieces of brick and mossy plants had caught in her intricately coiffured hair, which had somehow remained immaculate on the undamaged side of her head.

John Thimble looked shaken when he straightened. "This be a bad day. What with that there snake missing, and now this. And I planted that edelweiss the other day. I'd best get back there and see if I can save 'em."

He wandered over to the windows, which creaked back and forth in the wind. "Delicate plants they be, that edelweiss. Don't know as if I can save 'em, but I'll try."

"Thank you, John," Cecily said quietly. "I'm sure you'll do your best."

He looked as if he wanted to say something else, then touched his cap and disappeared into the dark, wet night.

"He seems more concerned about his plants than poor Lady Eleanor," Cecily said, getting up to lock the windows behind him.

"John cares very much for his gardens," Baxter said, opening the drawer of the sideboard. "He tends to his plants as if they were his children. I'm afraid he views the human species with less enthusiasm."

"Yes, I know what you mean." She watched Baxter spread a white tablecloth over the body. "I've sent a maid up to the Danburys' room. Robert Danbury should be here any minute. I'd appreciate it if you'd stay with me until he leaves."

"Of course, madam." Baxter straightened and tugged at the hem of his waistcoat.

Cecily sank into a chair at the head of the table. "The news will spread fast, I'm afraid. Soon everyone will know that one of my most prominent guests fell to her death because of my negligence."

"I don't think that is the case, madam. I erected the warning sign myself. The danger was quite clearly marked."

"Obviously it wasn't enough." Cecily tapped the polished mahogany with her fingernails. "I should have been aware of the problem before it could become dangerous. I should have had the wall inspected after that last bad storm. It's been catching the brunt of the wind and rain for over a hundred years. I should have known better."

She rested her chin in her hands, and studied the image of her dead husband. Was it her imagination, or did his smile of approval seem less broad?

"I would suggest that it was my duty to inspect the premises, not yours. If anyone is to blame, it is I."

"Piffle. James always stressed the importance of an owner taking care of his own property. You are here to run the hotel, not to maintain it."

"Forgive my humble opinion," Baxter said quietly, "but neither of us can be blamed for another's carelessness. If someone ignores a blatant warning, she should expect to pay the price."

"Thank you, Baxter. I'll attempt to keep that in mind."

"Yes, madam."

Cecily studied the roses. "I wish he hadn't had to leave so soon. He would have known how to deal with this." The lump in her throat stopped her for a moment. Recovering, she added softly, "I miss him so much."

"Yes, madam. I know."

She raised her gaze to Baxter's square face. "There are times, Baxter, when I wonder if I've taken on too much. But James used his last breath to tell me to hold on to the Pennyfoot. How can I not uphold his last wish?"

"I know he would be most proud of you. You have no reason to reproach yourself."

"I wish I could be so certain of that." Once more she rested her gaze on the roses.

"I would be happy to take care of Mr. Danbury, if you would rather."

She smiled and shook her head. "No. This tragedy happened in my establishment, and I have to accept the responsibility of dealing with it." She straightened her back as a sharp tattoo sounded on the door.

Baxter crossed the carpet swiftly to open it, and Cecily braced herself. This was likely to be extremely unpleasant. She could only hope that Robert Danbury would not lose his composure. She had seen a man weep only once, when James had cried in her arms after the death of their firstborn. She had found it most distressing.

The craving for one of her cigars was almost overwhelming. Not for the first time she wished that propriety allowed her to smoke in public. She had begun the habit soon after James had died, partly out of curiosity, and partly rebellion.

If she were to embark on this strange new life that James had so heedlessly heaped on her, she had told herself, she might as well start by establishing her independence.

At this particular moment, she needed that confirmation. She folded her hands and waited.

"Mercy me, whatever's happened," Mrs. Chubb exclaimed, hurrying toward the trembling Phoebe. "You look terrible."

Phoebe must have felt terrible, as her mouth opened and shut, but nothing came out.

"Gertie," Mrs. Chubb snapped, "help me get her to a chair, quickly. She looks like she's going to faint any minute."

Gertie dropped her sewing and heaved herself to her feet. "Blimey, she don't 'alf look a blinking mess."

"Gertie, fetch my smelling salts." Mrs. Chubb grabbed hold of Phoebe's arm. She was soaking wet and as cold as a dead fish. The arm hung limply, offering no resistance, and Mrs. Chubb peered into Phoebe's eyes. "Come on, duck. Come and sit down. I'll make you a nice cup of tea."

"I wet my drawers," Phoebe said in a high-pitched voice quite unlike her own.

Mrs. Chubb gasped. "What?"

"I wet my drawers," Phoebe wailed, and promptly burst into tears.

A loud snort exploded from Gertie, and she slapped her hand over her mouth, her shoulders shaking.

Mrs. Chubb dumped Phoebe hurriedly into the chair and grabbed the sniggering housemaid by the arm. Propelling her to the door, she rapped out, "Go and find Ethel and tell her to get along here at once, you hear me?"

Gertie nodded, her lips clamped tight on her grin.

Mrs. Chubb cracked out another order. "You keep your mouth shut about this, Gertie Brown. If I hear one word from anyone else, you'll be short a week's wages. I'll make sure of it. Do you understand?"

Gertie nodded again, then rushed through the door. Her raucous laughter followed her all the way down the hall.

Phoebe sat moaning, swaying back and forth as if she rode a rocking horse. She sat back with a gasp fast enough when Mrs. Chubb waved the bottle of smelling salts under her nose.

"There, duck, that'll do you. Now sit there while I fetch the tea."

Dying to know what could possibly have sent Phoebe into such a dither, Mrs. Chubb whisked into the kitchen and filled the kettle with water. She dumped it on the stove, then grabbed the poker and opened the doors to give the coals a hefty stirring. Sparks flew as the flames leapt in protest.

Satisfied, she slammed the doors shut and went in hunt of the chef's best brandy. She knew all the hiding places and found the half-empty bottle just as the kettle began to sing. Before long she had two steaming cups of tea, one of them fortified with a strong dose of cognac.

Returning to the sitting room, she found Phoebe staring into space, her hat a trifle lopsided, her hands beating a ceaseless tattoo on the arms of the chair.

Thoroughly alarmed, Mrs. Chubb held the cup and saucer in front of Phoebe's face. "Here, duck, swallow this. You'll feel much better when you've drunk it."

To her relief Phoebe came out of her trance and took the cup. After stirring the tea with a shaky hand, she took a sip. Then another. After a moment the frozen look thawed from her face, and a glow of appreciation crept over it.

She finished the tea with a gulp and set the cup and saucer down. "That was good, Altheda. Very good indeed. I feel much better. Thank you."

"My pleasure, dear," Mrs. Chubb assured her. "Now, how about telling me what's happened to get you in such a state."

Phoebe did, in graphic detail, with Mrs. Chubb hanging hungrily on every word.

"Go on!" Mrs. Chubb exclaimed when Phoebe had struggled to the end of her horrific tale. "Lady Eleanor. Well, I never."

Phoebe, warmed to a pleasant state of drowsiness by the brandy, nodded. Usually a lady of her background would not be exchanging confidences with a mere housekeeper, but Phoebe's sensibilities had gone through some drastic changes. Mrs. Chubb, or Altheda, as Phoebe called her in private, had been there when she'd badly needed a friend. And Phoebe never forgot a kindness. Or a slight for that matter.

"It was simply awful, I tell you," she said, hunting for her handkerchief in her soiled handbag. "Oh, my, I shall have nightmares for weeks."

"Yes, I'm sure you will." Mrs. Chubb looked up at the clock on the mantelpiece. "So what are you going to do about Henry, then?"

Phoebe blinked. "Henry?" She gasped, covering her mouth with her hand. "Henry! I'd forgotten about him in all this distress. He's still out there somewhere. Oh, Altheda, whatever shall I do?"

CHAPTER

❀6❀

"I just can't imagine how Henry managed to escape," Phoebe said, picking up her cup to examine it, as if she hoped to find more brandy in it.

"Well, I can tell you that." Mrs. Chubb rubbed her palms together, wishing she could repeat the sensational story to the ladies at the next church social. They'd be all agog, they would, and she'd be the center of attention.

They were always asking her about the goings-on at the Pennyfoot. Most of the time she'd had to keep her mouth shut. There were some things that she wouldn't tell her own mother.

She did wonder how madam was going to keep this one a secret. A death wasn't exactly the same thing as what went on behind the closed doors of the boudoirs. Maybe she'd get the chance to tell about it after all.

She started when Phoebe said, "So, please, do tell me. I would really like to know."

"It was Ethel. Countess Duxbury spilt a cup of tea all over the bed linens, and Ethel went to fetch clean ones. She was on her way out, and she says the snake lifted his head from the basket."

Mrs. Chubb chuckled. "What she meant was she got curious and peeked inside the basket to see what was there. She saw what was there all right. Shouldn't laugh, poor lamb, got such a fright, she did. Thought she was seeing things. She must have run out and left the door open. Never said a word until she overheard John say as how he'd been looking for a snake."

Phoebe moaned. "Oh, dear, I just don't know what I'm going to do."

"Well, duck, I should think you'll have to find him, won't you? I mean, we can't have a dirty great python slithering all over the place, can we? Wouldn't look good for the hotel, now, would it?"

"No," Phoebe agreed mournfully, "it wouldn't. But where do I look? John and I looked everywhere. The courtyard was the last place to look." She covered her eyes with her hands. "Oh, I'll never forget the sight of that poor woman lying there, those beautiful clothes all wet and bloody . . ."

Mrs. Chubb tried to be as diplomatic as possible. "Speaking of clothes, duck, yours could do with a wash." She thought for a moment. "What if I send you home to the vicarage with Ian in the trap? You could change your clothes and be back in plenty of time for the tableau. It's only ten past nine."

"Yes, I suppose that would be best." Phoebe sighed. "I suppose I'll have to tell Algie the whole story. He'll be most upset." She looked up at Mrs. Chubb with worried eyes. She'd refused to take off her hat, and it had dried out, though the brim still drooped in oddly shaped curves.

That was one hat, Mrs. Chubb thought, that would never look the same again. She'd never seen Phoebe without a hat. The reason for that wasn't ever mentioned between them, but Mrs. Chubb rather suspected that Phoebe's immaculate coiffure wasn't what the Good Lord had given her.

Not that there was anything wrong with wearing a wig. After all, the Society ladies all wore hairpieces to make their hair stand up in the front.

But Phoebe would be aghast if she thought her little deception had been unveiled, and Mrs. Chubb was the last person in the world to deny a woman her vanity. Lord knows they had little enough else left to enjoy.

"I wouldn't worry about the vicar, love," she said kindly. "He must have a lot of dealings with death and the like."

"Yes, but usually they are due to old age or disease. Algie never could stomach violent death." She dropped her voice to a confidential whisper. "He has a delicate stomach, you know."

It was Mrs. Chubb's considered opinion that everything about the Reverend Algernon Carter-Holmes was decidedly delicate, but she refrained from saying so.

There were enough whispers around the village about the vicar's soft lisping voice, which made it difficult to hear his somewhat diluted sermons. Mrs. Chubb used to get quite tired of her Fred digging her in the ribs, whispering harshly, "Wha'd he say?"

"I'm sure he'll live, dear," she assured Phoebe. "Now, wait there while I go and fetch Ian."

She patted Phoebe on the shoulder, just as the door opened behind her. Looking up, Mrs. Chubb saw Ethel's white face peering at her round the edge of the door. "You wanted to see me, mum?"

Mrs. Chubb nodded grimly. "You're late, where have you been?"

The door opened wider, letting in the rattle of dishes from the kitchen as Ethel shuffled into the room. Her thin shoulders were hunched, as if she were cold, and her face looked pinched and drawn. "I had to go and tell Mr. Danbury that Mrs. Sinclair wanted to see him in the library."

Phoebe gave a little moan, and Mrs. Chubb sent her a sharp look of warning. The less people who knew about the accident for now the better. "I see. Well, Gertie's in the kitchen with the dishes, so go and help her. I'll be in there in a jiffy."

"Yes, mum." She turned to go, and automatically Mrs. Chubb's critical gaze ran over her. "Here, wait a minute. What's that all over your shoes?"

Ethel lifted her skirt and examined her feet. Her white shoes were streaked with dirt. "Oo, look at that. Must have stepped in all that dirt on the landing upstairs."

Mrs. Chubb bristled. "What dirt?"

Ethel squatted down and wiped her shoes with the hem of her skirt. "Up on the third floor. By the roof staircase. Someone knocked one of them big plant pots over, and there's dirt all over the floor. I didn't have time to clean it up, but I'll go back and do it now, shall I?"

Phoebe let out a muffled squeak.

Ignoring her, Mrs. Chubb shook her head. "No, Gertie will be swearing like a fishwife if you don't get on in there and help her. I'll take care of the dirt. Go on then, look sharp!"

Ethel fled, and Mrs. Chubb looked at Phoebe, who seemed ready to burst into tears again. "What's the matter now?"

"Henry," Phoebe said, holding the brim of her ruined hat with both hands as she swayed from side to side. "He's inside the hotel somewhere."

"Oh, mercy, I hope not." Mrs. Chubb slapped a hand to her bosom. "What makes you think that?"

"I don't know for certain." Phoebe got wearily to her feet. "But I do believe that he might be responsible for that overturned plant pot. It would explain why we were unable to find him in the gardens. I just can't imagine how he got up to the third floor without being seen."

"Well, if you're right," Mrs. Chubb said, "I hope to high heaven we find him before someone else comes across him. Or we might have another death on our hands tonight."

"Please," Phoebe said faintly, "don't even think of it."

"Tell you what." Mrs. Chubb opened the door. "Stay here while I fetch Ian, and I'll have him run you home. While you're getting changed, I'll find Madeline, and we'll both look for Henry. You know how she is with animals—if anyone can find him, she will. And she'll know what to do with him when she does."

Phoebe sent her a grateful smile. "Thank you, Altheda. I greatly appreciate your kindness tonight."

Mrs. Chubb nodded and was about to leave when Phoebe gave a slight cough. "Er . . . Altheda?"

"Yes?" Mrs. Chubb waited, wondering what was coming next.

"You . . . ahem . . . you won't mention my little, er, incident to anyone?"

"Not on your life, duck."

"You don't think Gertie . . . ?"

"More'n she dare do. Don't give it one more thought. That'll be our little secret." Mrs. Chubb smiled, lifted her finger to her lips, then left in search of the footman.

"I've got a secret you'd love to know," Ethel announced when she joined Gertie at the sink.

Annoyed with her for being late and leaving her to get on with things by herself, Gertie snapped, "I couldn't care less. Get your hands in the bloody water and let me dry for a change. Me blinking hands are all shriveled up, they are."

"Well, all right. But this is a really special secret."

Gertie eyed her suspiciously. The girl looked ready to burst, she did. Intrigued in spite of herself, Gertie said casually, "So tell me, if it's that juicy."

"Can't." Ethel put a look of importance on her face. "Not supposed to gossip, are we?"

"Shit. Don't know why I bother listening to you." Gertie jerked her hands out of the water and reached for a tea towel.

"I wish I could tell you," Ethel wailed, looking as if she would explode if she didn't, "but I can't."

"Course you can." Gertie finished drying her hands, then reached out and pinched Ethel's lips. "Just open and shut these bloody things, and the words come out."

Ethel jerked back her head. "And you know I'll be in dead trouble if I do tell you."

Her curiosity thoroughly aroused now, Gertie scowled. "Oh, for Christ's sake, Ethel, spit it out. You know you're dying to tell me."

To Gertie's intense frustration, Ethel gave a firm shake of her head. "No. Me lips are sealed. More'n me life's worth to tell you."

"Strewth, Ethel, you really get my goat, you do. Whatcha say anything for if you aren't going to tell me?"

The other girl sighed. "Wish I hadn't said anything now."

Glaring at her, Gertie played her trump card. "All right. What if I told you I had a big secret, too? Something you'd love to know."

"Yeah? What is it, then?"

"You tell me yours and I'll tell you mine."

Ethel frowned. "How do I know yours is as big as mine?"

Her patience gone, Gertie dug her fists into her hips and yelled, "Are you bleeding going to tell me or not?"

"Sshh!" Ethel looked around at the door, as if expecting Mrs. Chubb to come barreling in there any minute. "All right." She leaned closer and whispered into Gertie's ear.

Blinking in surprise, Gertie listened to the whispered words, then drew her head back. "You're bloody daft. How can it be him?"

"I tell you it *is* him," Ethel hissed, plunging her hands into the soapy water. "I ought to know what he looks like. Seen his picture often enough, haven't I?"

Gertie lifted a stack of dirty plates and dumped them into the sink. "Go on. He wouldn't show his face down here. Be bloody stupid to do that, wouldn't he? Everyone gawking and staring at him? Blimey, the newspapers would have a right blast with that one, wouldn't they?"

"Well, all I can say is how I seen him, plain as a spot on your face."

"Yeah? What was he doing then? Stuffing his kite full of lobster, I suppose." She looked at Ethel's indignant face and exploded with laughter. "Gawd, Ethel, you don't half fall for 'em, don't you? Course it weren't him. Bet yer tuppence it weren't."

Ethel's face brightened. "All right. You're on. Bet you tuppence it is him."

Gertie stared at her, the plate she held dripping water over her shoes. It wasn't like Ethel to risk her hard-earned money unless she was on a sure thing. Maybe Ethel knew something she didn't.

Ethel gave her a triumphant smile. "See? Not so cocky now, are you?"

Stung, Gertie tossed back her head. ''All right, Miss Clever Sticks, how're you going to prove it?''

''All you got to do is look at him and you'll know.'' She held out a hand, slathered with soap suds. ''So, you going to shake on it?''

For a moment Gertie was almost convinced. Then common sense kicked in. ''Christ, Ethel, I'm blinking certain he ain't going to stay at the Pennyfoot. He goes to the bloody Riviera for his holiday, don't he? What would he be doing down here in this hole?''

Ethel shrugged. ''How do I know? P'raps he's brought one of his lady friends down here, 'coz no one would suspect him of being here.''

''They get an eyeful of him, they'll suspect all right.''

''And if he don't come out of his room, how're they going to see him?''

Still wavering, Gertie thought it over. No, it weren't possible. Not him. ''All right,'' she said, grasping the slippery hand and giving it a firm shake, ''I'll bet yer tuppence. What room's he in?''

Ethel told her. ''If you get caught snooping, though, you'd better not tell on me. You know as how we're not supposed to gossip. I could get the sack for telling you, I could.''

''I won't tell. God's honor.''

''All right, now it's your turn. What's your secret?''

Gertie smiled. ''Well, you know that old fart Mrs. Carter-Holmes? Well, you'll never guess in a million years what she did tonight . . .''

Cecily's heart went out to Robert Danbury as he gazed down at his dead wife. Dressed in the military uniform he'd obviously planned to wear to the ball, he stood with his hands clasped behind his back, his face pale and set.

She knew only too well how it felt to lose a loved one. The pain still haunted her unbearably during the long, empty hours of the night. ''I'll leave you alone with her, if you like,'' she said softly.

''That won't be necessary.'' Danbury visibly squared his

shoulders, then looked at Cecily. "Can you tell me what happened?"

"I'm afraid we don't know for sure. John Thimble, our groundskeeper, found her lying on the rockery in the courtyard. It appears she must have fallen through the wall of the roof garden, since several of the bricks lay shattered on the ground around her. I am so very sorry."

"I see." He lifted his chin a fraction. "I take it you've sent for the constable?"

"Yes. Police Constable Northcott and Dr. Evans will be here in the next hour or two. They have to come from Wellercombe—"

"Yes, I know." He stared dispassionately down at the body, as if afraid to allow himself the luxury of emotion. "I shall have to make arrangements, of course. It is too late tonight. I assume it will be in order to leave her . . . the body here until the morning?"

"Yes, of course." Cecily felt an urge to touch his arm in sympathy. He would have been horrified, of course, if she'd indulged the impulse. "Again, Mr. Danbury, I am most sorry. Having recently suffered a bereavement myself, I can well understand your distress at this moment."

Danbury lifted his head and stared at her. For just a brief moment, she saw anger in his pale blue eyes before he masked it. "Can you, Mrs. Sinclair?"

He dropped a last glance down at his wife, then with a nod of dismissal strode to the door. Reaching it, he turned. His voice sounded flat, devoid of emotion. "I'll be in my room. Please send the constable up to me at his earliest convenience."

"Yes, Mr. Danbury. Of course. And what about Miss Morris? Shall I inform her?"

He hesitated for a long moment, then said quietly, "No. I'll take care of it."

"Very well Mr. Danbury. As you like."

Cecily let out her breath as the door closed behind him. "Poor man. I'm glad that's over." She sank onto the chair and looked at Baxter, who had remained at a discreet distance throughout.

He moved forward now, to stand at the foot of the table. "Are you all right, madam?"

"What? Oh, yes. Thank you." She rubbed a hand across her brow. "I wonder if he'll bring charges against the hotel."

"I certainly would hope not, madam."

He'd sounded shocked, and she gave him a rueful smile. "You didn't see the look in his eyes just before he left. I'm afraid he might very well be vindictive." She sighed heavily, seeking comfort from the delicate colors of the roses. "Not that I would blame him, of course. If the wall had been sound, Lady Eleanor would still be alive."

"If milady had heeded the sign, she would not have fallen."

Cecily shrugged. "I fear it is a little late to play with ifs and if nots." She paused for a moment or two, then decided she could stand it no longer. "Bax, do you happen to have one of those wonderful little cigars you always carry around with you?"

Baxter switched his disapproving gaze to a point above her head. "Yes, madam."

"May I have one, please?"

"Madam, I don't think—"

"I know what you don't think. That doesn't alter the fact that I very much need one right now."

"This is most improper, and I object very strongly to encouraging you—"

"Baxter, if I were a man, would you not be happy to give me a cigar?"

He shifted from one foot to the other. "I need hardly point out that you are not a man, therefore the argument does not stand."

"Piffle. That is indeed what this argument is about. There is nothing to prevent me from going to my suite and smoking one of my own cigars."

"Yes, madam. Master Sinclair would be appalled if he were to see you."

"No doubt. But since he is the reason I indulged in this habit in the first place, if he were still here I would not be smoking. So can we now end this dispute?"

With wry amusement she watched the struggle go on inside

him. Finally he slipped two fingers into the pocket of his waistcoat and drew out a narrow, slim package. Without a word, he opened the end of it and handed it to her.

Cecily took it and withdrew one of the slender cigars, then handed the package back to him. "You have my permission to smoke, too, Baxter."

His face registered his discomfort. "Thank you, madam, but I prefer to wait until I am in my quarters."

Cecily sighed. How sad it was that convention disallowed them to be true friends. She genuinely respected his loyalty to the old regime, but at times it could be extremely tiresome.

She stuck the cigar in her mouth, leaned forward, and mumbled, "Then be so kind as to put a light to mine."

With a look of extreme distaste, he did so.

"This will not look good for us, Baxter," Cecily said gloomily, watching the smoke curl lazily up to the ceiling. "The hotel will have a smear against its name. You know how people love to gossip."

"Not the staff, madam."

"Of course not the staff. I have complete faith in their loyalty. I meant the guests. Once word of this dreadful accident travels around Mayfair, the Pennyfoot's name will be sullied."

Baxter opened the door of the sideboard and pulled out a silver ashtray. "Perhaps it was not an accident."

Cecily looked up sharply. Something in his voice had given her a quivery feeling in her stomach. "What do you mean?" she demanded, dreadfully afraid she already knew.

CHAPTER

❧ 7 ❧

Baxter crossed the room and laid the ashtray in front of Cecily. "Milady could have jumped."

"Jumped?"

"Thrown herself off the roof, madam."

Uneasily she tapped cigar ash into the ashtray. "Well, I know what you meant, but . . ." She resisted the urge to look at the body. "I don't really think Lady Eleanor is the kind of person to do that, do you?"

"Who knows which of us could be desperate enough to take our own life?"

"I would certainly hope she did no such thing. I find that unforgivable. Too many good people have lost their lives far too early because of disease or accident. Some people never fully recover from the loss of someone they love."

Baxter said nothing, but she knew he was aware she was thinking of James. After a pause she added, "Being a military

54

wife, I understand there are times when it is unavoidable to take the life of another. Even so, in my heart I cannot condone it. And to deliberately end a life needlessly, whether your own or that of someone else, is beyond my comprehension. The very thought of it fills me with rage.''

She thought about the aggressive, sharp-tongued woman she'd encountered on more than one occasion. "No, I don't believe Lady Eleanor would do such a thing. Though it would certainly present the misfortune in a more favorable light if it were so.''

"There is another possibility, madam.''

"And that is?'' She drew on the cigar, enjoying the sharp, acrid smell of the smoke. As a child she had often wondered what enjoyment could possibly be derived from such an odd habit that seemed reserved solely for the men. Now that she had taken up the habit herself, she had to admit the whole effect was undoubtedly soothing.

"It has been my contention, madam, that when one falls from a great height, it could be attributed to three possibilities. One either accidentally falls, or deliberately throws oneself off, or . . .'' He paused, obviously for effect. "Or one is pushed.''

Cecily coughed, choked, then coughed again, until tears ran down her cheeks.

Baxter tutted loudly. "Forgive my impertinence, madam, but smoking is not a habit a well-bred lady should acquire. It is likely to be the death of you.''

"Piffle.'' Cecily dropped the cigar into the ashtray and groped in her skirt pocket for her handkerchief. "Are you suggesting . . .'' The words came out in a hoarse croak. She took several deep breaths, while Baxter watched anxiously.

"Can I get you some water, madam?''

She shook her head fiercely, cleared her throat, and tried again. "Are you suggesting that someone murdered Lady Eleanor?''

"No, madam. I merely presented it as a possibility.''

Cecily stared at him. "Now that I think about it, it does seem peculiar. Why would she go up to the roof garden alone, and fully dressed for the ball? It must have been quite difficult to mount those narrow stairs, given the width of her padded skirts.''

''Precisely, madam.''

A chill crept down her back as she thought about it. ''Baxter, I'm not certain that a murder at the Pennyfoot would be any better than an accidental fall.''

''No, madam. One cannot be charged with negligence in the case of a murder, however.''

''True. But who would want to murder Lady Eleanor?''

''That I couldn't say.''

Cecily frowned. ''I do wonder where Mr. Danbury was while his wife was on the roof.''

''I believe he was in the gardens. I saw him leave the foyer a little after the grandfather clock chimed a quarter to seven.''

''That's right. Now that you mention it, I remember seeing him make for the stairs about ten minutes before John and Phoebe came to tell me about the accident. I didn't take too much notice as my attention was on Colonel Fortescue.''

She looked up at Baxter. ''What do you suppose Robert Danbury was doing out there in the rain?''

Baxter ran a finger around his stiff white collar. ''It's possible he had a rendezvous, madam.''

She pretended to be shocked. ''With a woman?''

''It is possible.'' Baxter gave her a look that said he knew perfectly well she was aware of the goings-on among her guests.

Cecily preferred to keep up the pretense, however. It eliminated the temptation to gossip, though it was difficult to ignore the rampant grapevine below stairs. ''I wonder what P.C. Northcott will make of all this?'' she murmured.

Baxter made a sound that sounded like ''Pshaw!''

Cecily had long been aware that Baxter and Stanley Northcott did not see eye to eye, though she had never known the reason for it. She'd once heard Baxter refer to the policeman as a bumbling fool with a lump of hog fat for a brain.

True, P.C. Northcott always took the path of least resistance, but then nothing much happened in Badgers End to get him excited. Cecily had the distinct impression that the constable was not the fool he appeared to be.

Although he lived in Wellercombe, seventeen miles away, that town was under the jurisdiction of Inspector William Cranshaw, who was much too involved with taking care of his busy borough to bother with the petty problems of Badgers End.

Which was why P.C. Northcott had been given the job of policing the village. This accident, happening as it did to a prominent member of Society, was most likely the biggest thing to happen to Stan Northcott in his brief career.

Cecily glanced at the clock gracing the mantelpiece. "Well, it will be a while yet before the P.C. arrives. I'm sure our conjectures are nothing more than flights of fancy, but perhaps I could ask a few questions before he gets here, just on the off chance I can find something a little more convincing than a mere possibility."

"I think that would be an excellent idea, madam."

She nodded, then pushed her chair back to rise. "I can't afford a scandal, Baxter. I can't afford to lose my customers. As I'm sure you're aware, it took every penny James had to finance the renovations for this hotel, and it will be years before the loans will be paid back. If it's at all possible that I can find something to help our case, I have to try."

Baxter leaned his hands on the table and fixed her with his dark brown gaze. "Madam?"

"Yes, Baxter?"

"You will take care?"

She smiled. "I would say I have more to worry about from Henry than I do a possible murderer, but I'll be on my guard. Now I want you to do something for me. That wretched snake has to be somewhere around, unless it has decided to go for a swim in the ocean. If so, we are likely to have another problem on our hands. In the meantime, I'd appreciate it if you would conduct a thorough search of the premises, as unobtrusively as possible, of course."

"Of course, madam."

She left him diligently cleaning the ashtray, and climbed the stairs to the third floor, wondering how she could be tactful about the questions she needed to ask.

*   *   *

Mrs. Chubb found Madeline in the conservatory, watering the tropical plants before she left for the day. Quickly she explained the dilemma. "Poor Phoebe will be most horribly mortified," she added, after filling Madeline in on the events of the past hour or two. "You know how much she puts into them tablets—"

"Tableaux," Madeline murmured, her mind obviously on another plane.

"Whatever you call 'em. Anyway, I said I'd ask you to help me look for him."

"I absolutely knew this was going to happen."

Mrs. Chubb looked at her suspiciously. "How'd you know?"

"I saw it quite clearly in the stars last night. I told Cecily this morning. A ring around the full moon, I said. I tried to warn her."

"Well, I don't know how the moon knew Henry was going to go missing, but ask it where the blue blazes he's hiding, will you?"

Madeline focused her gaze on Mrs. Chubb. "I'm not referring to the snake. I'm talking about Lady Eleanor."

"Oh, that." Mrs. Chubb nodded her head. "Yes, very sad that. But first things first, I say. The lady is dead, poor thing, but Henry is still very much alive, as far as we know, and if we don't find him soon he's going to get hungry." She paused, folding her arms across her chest. "And you know what that means."

"I do hope he doesn't attack the cats. I'm quite sure one of them is a reincarnation of Sir Francis Drake. He has such a fascination with water, you know. So unusual for cats."

Mrs. Chubb huffed her disapproval. "Are you going to help me look for him or not?"

Madeline sighed. "Oh, very well. I suppose my dinner can wait. But I insist on a snack first, or I shall positively faint from hunger." She floated off, followed by Mrs. Chubb, who couldn't help thinking that Madeline could do with a good meal to fatten her up.

* * *

Sounds of laughter, accompanied by the sprightly strains of a polka drifted up behind Cecily as she mounted the stairs. She thought uneasily how out of place the music seemed, given the circumstances.

Her light tap on the Danburys' door went unanswered, and she rapped her knuckles a little harder. After a long pause a voice asked curtly, "Who's there?"

"It's Mrs. Sinclair, Mr. Danbury. I wonder if you would do me the courtesy of answering a question or two?"

Another long wait, then the door opened abruptly. Robert Danbury looked displeased and somewhat disheveled. He'd changed out of his uniform, his dark hair was mussed, and he'd apparently donned his jacket in a great hurry, as one button remained unfastened.

Stepping out into the hall, he closed the door behind him. "What is it you want to know, Mrs. Sinclair?"

"I was wondering if you've spoken to Miss Morris, and if there's anything I can do?"

His eyes narrowed. "I have informed Miss Morris of her mistress's death. She has taken it well, under the circumstances, and is resting at the moment."

"Yes, well, perhaps I should look in on her, just to be sure."

He gave a clipped nod of his head. "As you wish." He moved his hand toward the door, and Cecily spoke quickly.

"Mr. Danbury, I was wondering why Lady Eleanor would have been in the roof garden by herself at such an hour. Especially since she was dressed for the ball."

Robert Danbury's hand hovered for a moment, then dropped to his side. "I'm afraid I can't help you with that, Mrs. Sinclair. Miss Morris was helping my wife prepare for the ball when I left to search for the dog. Miss Morris had taken it for a walk earlier, and it had slipped its lead. When I returned to the room, my wife had already left. I assumed she had become tired of waiting and had decided to accompany one of our acquaintances to the ball."

"You found the dog?" Cecily asked, trying to remember if he had it with him when she saw him earlier.

"Not at that time. Miss Morris brought the dog to my room

a little while later. She had managed to find him in the gardens. After she left I changed into my uniform for the ball. I was about to leave myself when I received your message.''

"I see." Cecily frowned. "Did Miss Morris not say why your wife had left?''

"She told me only that she had left Lady Eleanor here in the room while she resumed the search for the dog." He raised his hand again to the door. "If you will excuse me, this has all been rather a shock."

"Of course. I'm sorry to have bothered you, Mr. Danbury. If there's anything I can do?''

"Nothing, thank you.'' He opened the door, and she turned to go.

Then, on an afterthought, she asked, "Was Lady Eleanor, by chance, depressed about something?''

Robert Danbury's dark eyebrows arched. "Depressed? My wife had absolutely no reason to be depressed. She had everything she wanted—money, friends, a loving husband— no, Mrs. Sinclair, my wife was not depressed. She did not throw herself from the roof of this hotel, if that is what you inferred. Rest assured of that. It was an accident, pure and simple, and I would hope you will not raise a question about that.''

Cecily nodded dutifully. "Of course, Mr. Danbury. I apologize if I have caused you added distress.''

He stared at her for a moment longer, as if trying to guage whatever lurked in her mind, then he closed the door with a sharp snap.

Wincing, Cecily headed back down the hall, intending to talk to Daphne Morris. She met Phoebe at the head of the stairs, who puffed and panted, holding her sides to regain her breath.

She'd changed her clothes and now wore an elegant evening dress in sky-blue. The material had an attractive cut pile of dark blue and white chrysanthemums, and her matching hat swept low across her face. The crown was hidden under layers of blue and white silk roses, with yards of white chiffon veiling.

In her usual daytime dress of a crisp white shirt and black skirt, Cecily felt quite dowdy in comparison.

Phoebe's fortunes had changed considerably for the worst since her husband's accident had left her widowed. The family of the Honorable Sedgeley Carter-Holmes had disowned the unfortunate woman and her son, having always regarded her as beneath Sedgeley's station, and Phoebe had been left with little more than her personal belongings.

She had kept the beautiful gowns and jewels, however, refusing to sell them no matter how impoverished she might become. Phoebe had never forgotten her brief period as an aristocrat and had taken great pains to maintain her figure in order to keep up appearances.

Eyeing Phoebe's wasplike waist, which appeared to cut her in half between her bulging bosom and padded hips, Cecily knew just how tight the older woman had pulled the laces of her corset.

Cecily was often tempted to throw out the detestable things. If she had her way, no woman would have to force her body into the uncomfortable contraptions. As it was, she could hardly wait to be in the privacy of her room where she could slip out of her own corset and breathe easily again.

Phoebe held up her hand in a plea as she struggled for breath. "Wait . . . Cecily. Something . . . must tell you."

Cecily waited, hoping Phoebe wanted to tell her she'd found Henry.

Phoebe waved her hand at the end of the hall. "Henry," she gasped.

"You found him?"

The other woman shook her head. "I think he's in the hotel somewhere. Overturned plant pot."

Cecily looked down the hall but could see nothing. "Where?"

"No." Phoebe dragged in some more air.

It was no wonder she couldn't breathe, Cecily thought irritably. That dress was so tight it looked ready to burst a seam.

"Altheda cleaned it up," Phoebe managed painfully. "But I think Henry might have knocked it over."

Cecily finally understood. "Oh, Lord. Which plant pot?"

"The one at the end of the hall. By the foot of the roof

staircase.'' She looked startled, as if realizing something for the first time. ''Cecily! You don't think he's on the roof, do you?''

Cecily wanted to think no such thing. And she certainly didn't need Phoebe fluttering around up there. ''No I don't see how he could get up there. I'm sure it's just coincidence. I'll look around, though, just in case. Have you searched the cellar yet?''

Phoebe shuddered. ''No, I have just this moment arrived back from changing my clothes. Perhaps Mr. Baxter will look there for me?''

Knowing how Baxter intimidated Phoebe, Cecily nodded. ''I'll ask him. Why don't you look in the conservatory? Henry could be fast asleep under the aspidistra.''

''Yes, yes, pythons like plants, I do believe. I'll look there.'' She gave a little worried shake of her head. ''I only hope some earnest young man isn't trying to impress a young lady in there. He might well have an opportunity he least expected.'' She turned tail and, clinging to the banisters, began carefully descending the stairs.

Cecily looked down the end of the hall. The door that led to the staircase lay behind a heavy green velvet curtain. In the shadows created by the gas lamps along the hall, it was easy to imagine that a python could be curled up behind it.

She tried to think of everything she'd heard about pythons. The only thing she could remember was that they killed their prey by squeezing them to death, which was not a comforting thought.

CHAPTER

8

Cecily knew she would find a hurricane lamp and matches in the small cupboard at the foot of the steps. That was on the other side of the door, however. She would have to sweep the curtain aside in order to open it.

Deciding that she had better get on with it, she crept forward, every nerve in her body poised for flight. How fast could a python move? She had seen one in the zoo once. It moved quite slowly, as far as she could remember, but it hadn't been planning on attacking anyone then.

Mr. Sims had said that Henry was quite docile, as long as he was in his basket with the dead mice the handler had provided. Cecily wished she'd thought to bring along a dead mouse. As distasteful as the thought was, it was infinitely preferable to being hugged to death by a python.

She almost tapped on Robert Danbury's door to ask him to take a look behind the curtain. She actually paused in front of the door before she changed her mind. The poor man had enough to contend with right now. Besides, if what she suspected about Lady Eleanor's demise proved to be true, the last person she wanted around was Robert Danbury.

She crept forward another foot or two, passing beyond the glow from the last lamp. What if Lady Eleanor had emerged from her room and had come face-to-face with Henry? What if then, having locked herself out of the room, the only means of escape was the roof? What if Henry had followed her up there?

Cecily's heart began thumping. Was it possible milady had backed away from the snake in an effort to escape, pressed against the wall, and toppled over? If so, this was far worse than a damaged wall. This could, indeed, mean disaster for the Pennyfoot.

She reached the curtain. The only sound she could hear was the faint hiss from the gas lamps. The ballroom was too far away, and no one else stirred in the upper levels of the hotel. The shadows were too deep to tell if a python lay stretched behind the heavy folds. There was only one way to find out.

Holding her breath, she stretched out her hand and twitched the curtain aside. Instinct caused her to spring back, out of striking distance. She felt decidedly foolish when the expected sight of Henry lying in front of the door failed to materialize. She was most thankful no one else was there to see her behaving like the namby-pamby women she despised.

Feeling a touch more brave, she approached the door again. There was still the roof to consider, of course. She would have to investigate. She was tempted to go back down for Baxter. The prospect of wandering up there alone in the dark, damp night was not a pleasant one.

"What are you?" she whispered fiercely under her breath. "A woman or a mouse? Here's your chance to prove your mettle, my girl." If she didn't want P.C. Northcott running around the hotel asking questions and causing an uproar without good reason she had to determine exactly what had happened, if possible before he arrived and drew his own conclusions.

Leaving the door behind her slightly ajar for a quick escape if necessary, Cecily found the hurricane lamp in the cupboard and lit it. Then, moving with caution, she climbed the stairs to the roof.

The moist air chilled her when she pushed the door open and stepped outside. Shivering, she wished she'd thought to throw a shawl around her shoulders. But then she hadn't planned on taking a midnight stroll under the stars.

Now that the storm had passed, white clouds scudded across the crescent moon, casting moving shadows down the slope of the roofs and over the length of the roof garden. A still sea breeze ruffled the honeysuckle and rustled the leaves of the rosebushes.

Looking across at the wall, Cecily could see through the uneven gap the lights from the cottages, twinkling like a rope of diamonds up the slope of the cliffs. Being able to see almost to ground level gave her an eerie feeling, and her stomach lurched at the thought of the sheer drop just beyond her feet.

Reluctant to move, she swung the lamp in a high arc over her head. Light danced and played over the half barrels that served as flower beds for the plants. Her hand shook at the thought of spying the python lying there. She would most likely drop the lamp and run, she thought.

She made herself look back at the ruined remains of the wall. The rain barrel rested against the end that was still intact. Luckily it hadn't gone over, too. It would have caused more damage to the courtyard floor.

Cecily swung the lamp away, then a thought struck her, and she turned it back. The light fell on the rain barrel again—and nothing else. The sign that she had so carefully crafted and Baxter had wedged so securely against the wall was no longer there.

It hadn't landed in the courtyard with Lady Eleanor. Of that Cecily was quite certain. She would most certainly have seen it if it had. Then where was it? Who could have removed it? It would have taken some effort to drag it out from behind the barrel.

She didn't want to go near the edge, close to that terrible emptiness where solid bricks should have been. But if the sign had somehow slid down behind the barrel, she wanted to know it.

Holding the lamp high in front of her, Cecily advanced toward the wall. Crouching down, she peered into the corner behind the barrel.

The voice came out of nowhere, directly above her head. "Madam! I really must insist—"

Cecily yelped and jumped to her feet, the lamp swinging wildly in her hand. "Baxter! If you creep up on me once more in that fashion, I shall not be responsible for my actions."

"I beg your pardon, madam, but it vexes me that you take it upon yourself to engage in such precarious ventures. Why did you not inform me of your intentions?"

"I didn't know what my intentions were, Baxter, and even if I had, I doubt that I would have informed you. I'm not made of eggshells, as I'm constantly reminding you. I don't need, nor do I want, your insistent watchfulness of my every move."

Baxter's chin rose a fraction. "May I remind you that Master Sinclair extracted a promise from me on his deathbed, madam? I was instructed to take good care of you. I am only attempting to keep that promise."

Cecily huffed out her breath. "I understand that, but even James was not so solicitous about my well-being that I was forever falling over him. I do believe there can be some compromise here."

Baxter's back looked ramrod-straight. "Please accept my apologies, madam. I do not mean to intrude. I only wish to protect you from possible harm."

Her annoyance evaporated. "And I don't wish to offend you, Bax. I really don't. You startled me, that is all."

"Yes, madam. I apologize."

"Accepted." Anxious now to make amends, Cecily gestured at the rain barrel. "What do you think of this? The sign seems to have disappeared."

He stared at the spot for several seconds. "It does indeed. I wonder where it could have gone? I don't remember seeing it on the ground."

"Neither do I," Cecily said grimly. "But if it isn't there and it didn't fall, there could be only one other explanation."

"Someone removed it."

"Exactly." Cecily stood the lamp on the ground and rubbed

her chilled arms with her hands. "But why would anyone do that, unless they wanted to conceal the danger?"

"I cannot think of a single reason."

The shiver that shook her body was not entirely due to the cold. "Your third possibility is beginning to look more feasible, Baxter."

"Yes, madam." He stooped to pick up the lamp at her feet. "I think it best that you go back indoors, if I am not being too presumptuous?"

She ignored his touch of sarcasm. "I think we can safely assume that Henry isn't up here. It amazes me how so many things appear to have vanished in one day. Lady Eleanor's brooch, a large and very live python, Colonel Fortescue's pith helmet, and now a five-foot sign. I wonder what will be next?"

"I wonder indeed, madam."

"I think we must find that sign, Baxter." She walked ahead of him to the door and waited for him to open it.

"I will do my best."

"P.C. Northcott still hasn't arrived?"

"No, madam. We're expecting him momentarily, however."

"Yes. I have to talk to Miss Morris. Perhaps she can explain why Lady Eleanor came up here. But first I think I'll go down to the kitchen and treat myself to a nice hot cup of tea."

"I think that is an excellent idea."

He opened the door for her, and she stepped through, smiling at him. "You see, I can take care of myself."

His "Yes, madam" sounded a trifle dry, but she refrained from comment. Her mind was on the missing sign.

She couldn't imagine where it could be, but she had a strong feeling that when they found it—if they found it, and depending on where they found it—some of the uneasy questions on her mind could very well be answered. She could only hope that the answers wouldn't prove to be even more disturbing.

Phoebe reached the bottom of the staircase just as the grandfather clock began to strike the hour of ten. Mercy. She was still shaken by the dreadful sight of poor Lady Eleanor, and now time was running out. She had no more than two hours before the tableau was due.

Oh, this was a bad night. Madeline and her omens had wished this tragedy down on their heads, that was for certain. A death, she'd said, and a death there was.

The only consolation Phoebe could find was that Madeline had mentioned only one death. One could only hope that meant that Henry would remain docile after all.

Though what she would do if she didn't find him, Phoebe thought, she couldn't imagine. The entire effect would be ruined. She'd gone to so much trouble, and now her masterpiece would be ruined. Simply ruined.

She was so engrossed in her disappointment she didn't see Colonel Fortescue until he materialized in front of her. He bent forward from the waist, his eyelids fluttering faster than a bee's wings. "I say, madam, you look ravishing tonight. Quite ravishing."

Phoebe looked at his quivering white mustache with repugnance. "If you will excuse me, sir, I am on an important mission."

The colonel brightened visibly. "Mission, you say! Jolly hockey sticks, what? Perhaps I might help?"

She stared at him thoughtfully. "Perhaps you might at that. You may help me hunt for Henry."

"Right! Hunt for Henry. Excellent campaign, madam. I'll embark at once." The colonel saluted, turned smartly on his heel, and began marching away.

Phoebe pursed her lips and waited.

He got a dozen steps away before he halted. Then he turned and marched back. "Incomplete orders, old bean. Dashed awkward. Need more information."

Phoebe slid the strap of her silk evening bag farther up her gloved arm. "Colonel Fortescue, during your commission overseas, did you by any chance ever come across a python?"

The colonel's eyes blinked even more furiously. "You m-m-m-m-mean a s-s-s-snake?"

"I mean a very large snake, Colonel."

"Well, by Jove, I know what one looks like." He looked right, then left, then leaned forward, his finger pressed to his lips. "I've got it. Password is python. Mum's the word! This Henry must be a big cheese, what?"

A startled look came over his face, and his cheeks grew even more crimson. "By George, madam, I do believe I know what this is all about."

Surprised by this unexpected intuition, Phoebe exclaimed, "You do?"

"Yes, indeed." He leaned closer, his eyes twitching in excitement. "It's that chappie in suite three, isn't it?"

Phoebe had a little trouble with that one. "Chappie?"

"Yes, you know. Him. The big one."

Phoebe was beginning to wish she'd never started this. "I really do not have the faintest idea what you are talking about, Colonel. Perhaps—"

She stopped short. The colonel had whispered a name. A name she recognized. Unable to believe her ears, she asked him to repeat it.

He did so. It still sounded the same.

"Are you sure?" she whispered.

The colonel nodded his head in time with his blinks. "Oh, yes, quite, quite. Saw him with my own eyes. Couldn't mistake him, old girl. Not something you see every day, what?"

"No, it isn't," Phoebe politely agreed. Silly old fool. Whatever would he come out with next? "But in any case, this has nothing to do with the gentleman in suite three."

"Oh." The colonel looked disappointed. "Then who are we talking about? Who is this Henry? Not a duke, is he? Can't abide dukes. Testy fellows, the ones I've met. No time for the military at all."

"Henry," Phoebe explained with remarkable patience, "is a python."

The colonel jumped back as if he'd touched a nest of ants. "Great Scott, madam! I can't go hunting all over India for a snake! No, by Jove, not cricket is that. Not cricket at all."

Phoebe leaned forward and tapped him delicately on the arm. "Sir, you don't have to travel all the way to India. Henry is somewhere in this very hotel. He escaped from his basket and appears to be hiding at the moment, but I'm sure someone with your experience can ferret him out in no time."

The colonel was so shocked he actually stopped blinking for a moment. "In this hotel?"

Phoebe nodded. "In this hotel. Perhaps you'd care to investigate the cellar?"

Colonel Fortescue snapped to attention. "Have no fear, madam. I will engage the enemy and secure his surrender." He leaned forward, blinking anxiously. "I say, what do I do with him if I find him? Slice off his head?"

Phoebe yelped in alarm. "No, for heaven's sake don't even touch him. Just make sure he can't escape again and then come find me. I will be in the conservatory. I'll take his basket down and tempt him back inside it with his dinner."

At least she hoped she'd be able to tempt Henry. Heaven knows what she would do if he refused to budge. Somehow the thought of actually touching the huge snake took away a lot of the urgency to find him. Maybe she should join forces with Altheda and Madeline.

"His dinner," the colonel repeated solemnly.

Phoebe nodded. "A dead mouse or two."

There was a long silence. Then the colonel straightened. "Ah. Enough said." He spun on his heel once more, drew an invisible sword, and muttered, "To arms, men! Fall in!" With that he charged across the foyer and down the staircase.

Feeling pleased with herself, Phoebe turned and headed for the conservatory.

CHAPTER

❀ 9 ❀

Mrs. Chubb met Cecily in the hall. "Oh, madam, am I glad to see you. When Phoebe told me you were on the roof, I near had a fit, I did. I sent Mr. Baxter up there right away."

"So that was how he knew I was there." Cecily smiled ruefully. With all this protection how could she possibly come to harm?

"Well, mum, I couldn't rest knowing as how you were up there in the dark, and that snake roaming around somewhere. Must be the accident giving me the jitters. I'm as jumpy as a kitten in a hayloft tonight."

"I think it's upset us all, Mrs. Chubb."

"Oh, I hope you don't mind, mum, but there's something I been meaning to ask you." She bent forward, put a hand up to her mouth, and whispered, "If I might ask, who's the gent staying in suite three?"

Cecily frowned. ''I really don't know. Baxter took the booking. Why, is there a problem?''

To her consternation, Mrs. Chubb looked most uncomfortable. ''Well, not exactly a problem, mum, you might say, but more of a question really. I mean, it's none of my business, of course, but as the housekeeper here, I think I should be made aware of any—''

''Mrs. Chubb. Will you please tell me whatever it is you are trying to say?''

''Yes, well, mum, Gertie asked me something that really surprised me. Says that Ethel knows 'cause she's seen him and swears on her soul that it's him.''

Thoroughly confused now, Cecily stared at the housekeeper's worried face. ''Who are we talking about?''

''The gent in suite three.''

''So I gathered. And who does Ethel think he is?''

Mrs. Chubb leaned closer and whispered a name.

Startled, Cecily drew back. ''I hardly think so. I'm quite sure Baxter would have informed me if that were true.''

Mrs. Chubb nodded. ''That's what I thought. Still, Ethel seemed so certain it was him. I hope to goodness it's not. Can you imagine him coming face-to-face with a snake in the hall? We'd all be shot on the spot, shouldn't wonder.''

Dismissing it as absurd, Cecily shook her head. ''Don't worry, Mrs. Chubb, I'm sure it's just a rumor, and you know how gossip spreads among the staff. I do wish you'd try to keep that down a bit more.''

Mrs. Chubb looked suitably contrite. ''Yes, mum. I do my best.''

''I'm sure you do. As for Henry, I really can't think where he can be. Is Phoebe still hunting for him?''

Cecily began walking toward the kitchen, and Mrs. Chubb followed her. ''Yes, mum. Madeline is, too. Though short of searching the guest rooms, I think they've covered just about everything by now. Phoebe says she's even got Colonel Fortescue searching the cellar. Though by now he's probably been into the gin and is most likely lying flat on his back, sozzled to the gills.''

"Well, that might be a good place for him right now. I've enough to worry about without running into him again."

Mrs. Chubb clicked her tongue. "I know exactly what you mean. Had Gertie searching for half an hour, he did, for his watch. Had it in his weskit pocket all along. Talk about a waste of time. I couldn't think where Gertie had got to. She said she met him on the way back from taking a message to Lady Eleanor, but—"

"Pardon?" Cecily stopped abruptly and spun around to face Mrs. Chubb. "What did you say?"

"I said I was wondering where Gertie had got to—"

"No. After that. About Lady Eleanor."

"Oh, yes. Well, a gentleman gave Gertie a message to take to Lady Eleanor and—"

"When was that?"

She'd tried very hard to sound calm, but Mrs. Chubb gave her a sharp look. "Oh, I think it would be around half past seven or thereabouts. Remember when you were looking for her to ask her about the brooch?" She rubbed her chin, looking thoughtful. "I reckon Gertie won't have to worry about that anymore, will she? Bit of luck for her."

"Yes," Cecily agreed, not really listening. "But about the message. Did she say who gave it to her?"

Mrs. Chubb shook her head. "No, but you can ask her. She's still in the kitchen, finishing up the dishes most likely." They reached the kitchen door as she spoke, and Mrs. Chubb pushed it open.

A cloud of steam enveloped the room, and it was a moment or two before Cecily saw Gertie and Ethel at the sinks, their faces red and perspiring, wisps of hair stuck to their foreheads.

Gertie chatted away, ten to the dozen, while Ethel dried the large Wedgewood vegetable dish she held, nodding halfheartedly now and again.

Gertie finished polishing a crystal brandy glass and twirled it between thumb and forefinger while she examined it. "Well, like I told him, I wasn't bleeding having none of it, I wasn't. Bloody sauce. What does he take me for, that's what I want to know?"

"Gertie!" Mrs. Chubb rapped out. "Madam wants a word with you."

Gertie jumped violently, fumbled with the glass, then grabbed it to her chest with both hands. "Strewth, that was bleeding close. Almost dropped the bugger."

"Well, it wouldn't be the first one, would it? Which reminds me, young lady. What about that jar of piccalilli in the larder?"

Gertie looked puzzled. "What jar?"

"The one on the shelf next to the button tin. You know very well what one I mean. It's lying smashed to smithereens on the floor of the larder, that's what one. Mustard pickle all over the place. A right mess that was to clean up I can tell you. You're lucky I didn't come in here and lead you by the ear back to the larder to clean it up yourself."

Gertie shrugged, her face growing a deeper shade of scarlet. "I don't know what you're talking about. I didn't smash no jar. Probably those blinking cats always jumping in and out the window, they are. Ain't my bleeding fault."

Mrs. Chubb opened her mouth to deliver a torrent of reprimand, but Cecily laid a restraining hand on her arm. "Perhaps you could make me a pot of tea, Mrs. Chubb, if it isn't too much trouble?"

Mrs. Chubb sent a look at Gertie that spoke volumes before answering. "Of course, mum. Have it ready in a jiffy."

Cecily smiled and turned to Gertie, who waited with an anxious frown on her sweat-sheened face.

"Why don't we step out in the hall for a minute," Cecily suggested, moving back to the door.

Gertie followed her out and stood there with her back against the wall, twisting the folds of her apron tighter and tighter around her fingers.

"Mrs. Chubb tells me you took a message up to Lady Eleanor's room, Gertie," Cecily said as the housemaid fixed her gaze on the carpet.

"Yes, mum. A gentleman gave me a note to give her."

"About what time was that?"

"Half past seven, mum. I heard the clock chime as I was climbing the stairs."

"I see. And was Lady Eleanor there when you got there?"

"Yes, mum. I gave her the note meself."

Cecily paused for a moment, her mind calculating the time. Robert Danbury had returned from the gardens about ten minutes before eight. John and Phoebe had arrived shortly after eight o'clock. That meant that in order for Lady Eleanor to have climbed the stairs to the roof and fallen to her death, she would have had to have left her room, without waiting for her husband, soon after receiving the note.

There was only one reason Cecily could think of for Lady Eleanor to leave in such a hurry. And that was if someone had sent a message asking milady to meet him.

She looked at the housemaid's downcast face. "I don't suppose you read the note, Gertie?"

Gertie looked suitably shocked. "What, me, mum? Not bleeding likely. I knows me place, I do."

Pity, Cecily thought wryly. "Well, perhaps you can tell me who gave you the note?"

Gertie shook her head. "Dunno who it was, mum. I couldn't see his face, like."

Cecily frowned. "You couldn't see?"

"No, mum. He was all dressed up for the ball, in his costume. Had a mask over his face. I think he had a cold, though. He sounded real horsey, like."

"Hoarse," Cecily murmured, without thinking.

"Yes, mum. Horsey. Like what pulls a cart."

"Gertie," Cecily said slowly, "can you remember what kind of costume the man was wearing?"

Gertie beamed. "Oh, yes, mum. That one's dead easy. Half the men what go to the costume balls wear 'em. He was wearing a soldier's uniform. Like they wear in the tropics. You know, with one of those funny helmets to keep off the sun, and white gloves and all."

"Should've seen madam's face when I told her," Gertie told Ethel, after Mrs. Chubb and Cecily had left the kitchen. "Talk about knock her down with a feather. She just stood there, staring at me like she was in a bleeding trance, she did. Then 'Thank you, Gertie,' she said, 'you've been most helpful.' Though I don't know what I did, I'm sure."

"Oo, heck. Wonder what's up?"

"Dunno. And I don't want to know." Gertie plunged the cups and saucers into the bowl. "It's all got to do with that Lady Eleanor's accident, shouldn't wonder. Shouldn't speak ill of the dead, I know, but if it had to happen to anyone, I'm glad it was her. She won't be accusing me of thieving no more, will she?"

"Wonder who he was? The bloke what gave you the note?"

Gertie shrugged. "Don't know and don't care. I tell you one thing, I ain't the only one who ain't crying me eyes out over what's happened. But from now on, I'm going to keep me bleeding mouth shut, then I can't get in no more trouble."

She didn't say so, but she had a feeling she was already in far more trouble than she could handle. She was glad when Ethel changed the subject.

"So go on telling me about Ian," Ethel said, industriously buffing a spoon with her cloth. "What happened after you had a go at him?"

"Oh, well, we kissed and made up, didn't we."

For once Ethel's shocked gasp failed to please her. Her mind was still on madam's questions. And the sinking feeling in the pit of her stomach that told her she had plenty more to worry about than her argument with Ian.

Daphne Morris's room, a much smaller version than her late employer's suite, was on the second floor. Cecily climbed the stairs slowly, her mind going over her conversation with Robert Danbury.

When he'd answered her questions, he'd made no mention of the message his wife had received. Either he didn't know or he'd kept that piece of information to himself.

Gertie said a man in uniform had given her the note. Robert Danbury had been wearing a uniform when he'd viewed his wife's dead body. But Cecily had seen him herself shortly before that, and he hadn't been wearing it then.

If Danbury was the person who gave the note to Gertie, why hadn't he simply delivered it himself? Why would he wear his uniform at half past seven, take it off again to look for the dog, and put it back on again at eight o'clock?

It didn't make sense. Besides, Baxter had seen him leave the foyer at a quarter to seven. So apparently he'd been in the gardens all that time. She herself had seen him enter the foyer around ten minutes to eight.

Cecily wondered if Daphne Morris knew about the message. She would be sure to ask her, she decided as she paused in front of Daphne Morris's door.

Miss Morris answered Cecily's knock almost immediately. Although she held a small lace handkerchief crumpled in her hand, and her face bore traces of tears, she appeared quite composed, much to Cecily's relief.

"Oh, Mrs. Sinclair. What a dreadful business this is. To fall from that height . . . poor Lady Eleanor. Such a tragedy."

"I'm very sorry, Miss Morris," Cecily said quietly. "I'm sure this must be a great shock for you."

Daphne Morris nodded. "Yes, naturally it is. A great shock." She appeared to struggle for words and finding none, made an empty gesture in the air with her hand.

Cecily watched her for a moment, feeling a deep sympathy for her. Sudden death was always so difficult to comprehend. But Daphne Morris had more than shock to deal with. She was also faced with the prospect of seeking new employment. Her future must look very bleak.

At her age she would find it difficult to obtain another position, especially one that afforded her such a comfortable living. Even if Lady Eleanor had made a will, it didn't seem likely she would leave her companion more than a token sum.

There were other jobs, of course, but most decent positions required experience, and a companion didn't have much of that. She would be considered too old to train in a new profession. The poor woman must be devastated.

"I'm sorry to bother you at this time," Cecily said gently, "but I wonder if I might come in for a minute or two? I have a question I'd like to ask you."

"Of course."

Cecily followed her into the room. Miss Morris had changed out of her day dress and now wore a comfortable tea gown. She was a tall woman, and the pale lemon chiffon suited her. She'd removed her corset, and the gown clung to her slender figure, flaring out to swish in gentle folds around a pair of frail ankles. A little short, Cecily noted, but a good quality material. Most likely passed on by Lady Eleanor.

Daphne Morris dabbed delicately at her nose with the handkerchief. "Please take a seat, Mrs. Sinclair. How can I help you?"

Cecily sat on a tufted-back armchair and waited until the younger woman had seated herself on the tapestry ottoman. When the woman looked at her expectantly, she began, "I was wondering, Miss Morris, if you would tell me when you last saw Lady Eleanor?"

Daphne Morris looked troubled, but answered readily enough. "A little before half-past seven. I had taken Chan Ying for his walk, and he'd slipped his lead. I couldn't find him, and so I returned to the Danburys' suite as it was nearing time for the ball."

She looked a trifle distracted for a moment, then with a slight shake of her head continued. "Mr. Danbury left to search for Chan Ying while I dressed Lady Danbury's hair. Then I left her in her room to wait for her husband while I went back to the gardens to look for the dog."

Cecily nodded. "You saw no one else in that time?"

The companion's gaze wavered, then she looked down at her lap, shaking her head.

This was not an enviable position to be in, Cecily thought unhappily, but she had to have some answers. "Miss Morris," she said quietly. "Shortly after half-past seven this evening, one of the housemaids delivered a message to Lady Eleanor. I was wondering if there is anything you can tell me about that."

She waited, hoping that Daphne Morris knew about the message and that her loyalty to her dead employer wouldn't prevent her from sharing that knowledge.

CHAPTER

✖ 10 ✖

Daphne Morris looked pale as she stared at Cecily. "Message? I'm sorry, I'm afraid I know nothing about a message. Who was it from? What did it say?"

Cecily sighed. "I was hoping you'd be able to tell me."

Miss Morris stared down at her hands. "Lady Eleanor was not in the habit of sharing her correspondence with me, Mrs. Sinclair. I was, after all, nothing more than her paid companion."

Cecily nodded. "Yes, but often a lady's companion knows more about her mistress's private life than milady's friends. As I said, I am anxious to find out as much as possible about the events leading up to the accident."

The companion remained silent, and Cecily added for good measure, "The constable will be here shortly and will want answers to his questions. I'm merely trying to save my guests any unnecessary inconvenience."

Daphne Morris dropped her gaze back to her lap. "I appreciate your concern, Mrs. Sinclair. You are most thoughtful, I am sure. Unfortunately I can't help you. As I said, I know know nothing of any message. If Lady Eleanor received one, it must have been after I left to search for the dog."

Frustrated, Cecily stared at Daphne Morris's bowed head. She couldn't help feeling that the woman was deliberately keeping something back. It seemed fairly certain that Lady Eleanor had received a message from a gentleman asking her to meet him. Did Daphne Morris know who that man was? Any one of a number of men would be wearing military uniforms to the ball.

It could have been Robert Danbury, of course, but that seemed extremely unlikely. But *someone* had sent that note. Whoever he was, he must have had a pressing and urgent reason to request a meeting with Lady Eleanor at that hour. And she had gone alone. At the request of the mystery man? If so, then it would seem that Baxter's suggestion was not as preposterous as it had at first sounded.

In fact, Cecily was aware of a growing conviction that Lady Eleanor's death had not been an accident at all. It seemed as if she could well have died by someone's hand. In all probability, a murderer still lurked somewhere around the hotel.

Phoebe had spent a precious twenty minutes peering nervously under the tropical plants, to no avail. Henry remained stubbornly missing. She finally had to give up the search when a young woman came whirling into the conservatory on the arm of a besotted gentleman, both of whom giggled and whispered, obviously wishing to be alone.

Phoebe felt a moment's pang of envy before scuttling from the room. It really didn't seem that long ago since she had existed in that happy state of affairs with dear Sedgeley.

Though what he would think of the world now, with all this to-do about women and their rights, she shuddered to think. Poor Sedgeley would be horrified by the antics of that Pankhurst woman, what with her being thrown in prison like a street urchin. And all this talk about reform. Goodness knows what good they thought it would do.

Reaching the foyer, she thought about going down to the cellar to see how Colonel Fortescue was doing. On second thought, she decided it wouldn't do to be alone down there unchaperoned, and heaven knew what the colonel had been into. What if he were drunk, for heaven's sake? He could have his way with her, and she would be helpless.

Phoebe considered the possibility with more interest than could be considered proper, then dismissed it. Definitely not the colonel. If she was going to be ravaged, she would much rather it was one of those dashing young men whirling around the ballroom floor at that very minute.

A little scandalized by her own audacity, Phoebe concentrated on the problem at hand. Time was running out fast. If she didn't find Henry in time for the tableau, it would have to proceed without him.

She had intended to have Henry coiled in his basket on top of a pedestal center stage, after having been fed, which, Mr. Sims had assured her, guaranteed his staying put.

Once the orchestra began playing "his music," Henry had been trained to raise his head and sway majestically back and forth until the piece ended, wherein he would retire once more to his red satin pillow.

Phoebe sighed. If Mr. Sims had not been called away on an emergency, he would have been there himself to handle Henry, and none of this would have happened. But it had happened, and she couldn't do much about it now.

The tableau wouldn't be nearly as spectacular without the python, of course, but short of climbing up there herself and doing a fan dance, she just couldn't come up with an alternative.

She could, of course, put the basket up on the pedestal and hope no one would notice Henry wasn't in it. She could always tell everyone afterward that he slept through the entire performance.

Delighted with herself for coming up with a reasonable answer to her problem, she hurried down to the kitchen. Perhaps, if she could find the girl, she could ask Gertie to retrieve Henry's basket for her.

Madeline was floating around the kitchen when she got

there, a sausage roll in one hand and gesturing vaguely with the other while spouting to Mrs. Chubb rubbish about bad spirits floating around the Pennyfoot.

"I can sense them, my dear," she declared as Phoebe came through the door. "The full moon always brings bad luck to those who have angered the spirits. Lady Eleanor must have been too, too naughty for words. She has paid the price for her misdeeds."

"Please don't let Cecily hear you say that," Phoebe said in a sharp voice. "We all have problems enough without listening to that stuff and nonsense tonight."

Madeline lifted a delicately plucked eyebrow. "Oh, don't worry, Phoebe," she said, her voice sounding just a shade condescending, "you have nothing to fear from them. They've claimed their victim for this night. You are quite safe, I assure you."

Irritated by all this mumbo jumbo, Phoebe tossed her head, flipping chiffon everywhere. Madeline had no right to speak to her like that. No right at all.

The woman might have her fancy speech, but if gossip were to be believed, it was merely thanks to a mysterious uncle who took her in when her parents supposedly died at sea. It was no secret—everyone knew that Madeline's blood was Romany. And no gypsy was going to speak to her in that tone.

"They used to burn witches at the stake, so I'm told," she retorted.

"And every one of them returns to haunt the disbelievers. Didn't you know that?" Madeline had a low, gurgling laugh that always sounded as if she had a bad cold.

Phoebe tossed her head in disgust. She would waste no more time arguing with this harlot. Some of the stories she'd heard about Madeline Pengrath would grow hair on Algie's head if she ever repeated them. Not that she could be so bold, of course. It would be enough to shock him to an early grave.

"I have a lot more to worry about tonight than ghosts and goblins," she said. "Henry is still missing, and the tableau is due to start in little more than an hour."

Mrs. Chubb tutted. "Can you believe a snake that size could be slithering around this hotel and no one can find him?

Wherever could he have got to? There can't be that many places to hide.''

Madeline perched a hip on the corner of the scrubbed oak table, ignoring Phoebe's scandalized frown. "Well, I can assure you of one thing, he's not in the gardens.''

"How do you know?" Phoebe demanded.

"Vibrations." Her hands fluttered in the air. "They are all around me, singing to me. Henry is inside the walls of this building, you may rest assured of that.''

In spite of herself, Phoebe cast a nervous glance around. "Is he in a good mood?''

Madeline smiled. "At the moment I do believe he is.''

Annoyed that she'd allowed herself to be caught up in Madeline's nonsense, Phoebe said testily, "Well, if he is, he must be invisible, that's all I can say. I have searched every possible nook and cranny for that snake. Every corner, every floor—''

"Every cupboard?" Madeline inquired softly.

Phoebe shut her mouth with a snap. "Cupboard?''

"Oh, my," Mrs. Chubb said, slapping a hand to her mouth, "you really think he's in one of the cupboards, then?''

"He's in an enclosed space, of that I am absolutely convinced." Madeline slid off the table and stood with her head tilted back, eyes closed, and one hand held out as if she were testing the air for rain. With her long hair streaming down her back she reminded Phoebe of a statue of a water nymph she'd seen in Kew Gardens in London.

"Well, if you're so clever," Phoebe snapped, miffed at this ridiculous waste of time, "then please inform Henry to get back here at once. He's late for the tableau. My dancing girls will be arriving any minute, and I have to set things up for their entrance on stage.''

Madeline opened one eye. "I'm afraid I can't do that. He's asleep. In any case, he can't get out. The door is shut.''

Mrs. Chubb was following the conversation with a look of intense fascination on her round face. "What door is that, then?''

"Yes, do please tell me, I would dearly love to know," Phoebe said, getting more irritated by the minute.

"I can't tell," Madeline murmured, drawing the words out in a mournful monotone. Closing her eye again, she hugged herself and swayed back and forth. "I know only that the door is closed."

"Oh, for heaven's sake." Phoebe straightened her hat with an angry jerk of her hands. "I've had enough of this." She turned to Mrs. Chubb. "I need some help carrying my equipment from the laundry room to the dressing room. There's the sedan chair for the sultan, and the pedestal . . ." She sighed heavily. "The pedestal which Henry should have adorned, and the box of costumes."

Mrs. Chubb smiled. "I'll see to it. Ian's on duty in the foyer. I'll get him to carry it in for you."

Phoebe nodded. "Thank you, Altheda. As soon as possible, if you please. With all this confloption going on, I'm desperately late as it is. My girls are most likely waiting to get dressed this very minute."

"A broom cupboard," Madeline announced loudly, startling the other women.

"What?" Mrs. Chubb exclaimed, while Phoebe clicked her tongue in exasperation.

Madeline opened her eyes and swept the air with her hand in a gesture of triumph. "Henry. I do believe he's in one of the broom cupboards."

"Which one?" Mrs. Chubb asked. "We've got one on each floor."

"I don't know that, I'm afraid. But I think you should start with the top floor and work down."

"May I ask," Phoebe said with deceptive politeness, "how Henry managed to get into the broom cupboard through a closed door?"

"Dearie, I really can't be expected to know every tiny detail." Madeline wiped her brow with the back of her hand, as if she'd toiled for an hour in the potato fields. "You know how too, too exhausted I get when I'm concentrating like this."

"Tell you what, Phoebe," Mrs. Chubb said, "why don't you take Madeline and look in the broom cupboards while I get Ian to fetch your stuff for the tableau? If Henry's there, well and good. We'll take his basket up to him, and Madeline can get him into it. If he's not there, then you'll just have to do without him, won't you?''

She didn't like it, Phoebe thought, but if Madeline proved to be right, much as she doubted it, and they discovered Henry, her problems would be solved. Apart from anything else, she was not looking forward to explaining to Mr. Sims that she'd lost his valuable snake.

"Very well," she said, "but we will really have to hurry." Remembering her conversation with the colonel earlier, she added casually, "By the way, Altheda, do you happen to know the name of the gentleman in suite three?"

She had expected surprise at her question, even resentment at her curiosity, but not for one moment had she expected the flood of color that swamped Mrs. Chubb's face.

For several moments the two women stared at each other, while Mrs. Chubb's mouth opened and closed like a trout stranded on a rock.

Then the housekeeper apparently found her voice. "Well, I'm sure I don't know, Phoebe. The maids take care of the rooms, as you know. I wouldn't know the names of anyone staying there."

Phoebe's heart took a little jump of excitement. She found Altheda's reaction most interesting. Most interesting indeed. "Yes," she murmured. "Well, we must get on for now. Come, Madeline."

Madeline glided across the floor to the door and pushed it open. "Of course," she said, "I'm not promising anything. But I do most definitely feel it strongly enough to warrant a search."

Forcing her mind back to the matter at hand, Phoebe hoped that whatever "it" was, it knew what it was talking about. A little grumpily, she followed Madeline up the stairs.

All this climbing about was bound to have an effect on her poor legs, she thought. She'd never be able to kneel on that hard church floor for the Sunday service, and then Algie would be upset with her.

"I was most intrigued by your question to Mrs. Chubb," Madeline said as they rounded the curve to the second landing.

"My question?" Phoebe asked innocently.

"The name of the gentleman in suite three?" Madeline's dark gaze flicked over Phoebe's face. "Is it someone you could be interested in, Phoebe? I'll be only too happy to help if it is. I have some wonderful potions that are most successful in arousing a man's interest. You simply have to find an opportunity to slip it into his morning cup of tea."

Phoebe's snort of disgust was most unladylike. "You really are impossible, Madeline. For someone who proclaims to have the ability to read minds, you are remarkably obtuse. This entire speculation is quite ludicrous, even for you."

Unaffected by this attack, Madeline waved a languid hand in the air. "Oh, pooh, Phoebe, whyever not? It happens all the time."

"At my age?"

"At any age. Are you sure you're not pining after some tall, dark, and handsome gentleman?"

Thoroughly embarrassed, Phoebe snapped, "If you knew who it is, or supposed to be, you wouldn't be so flippant with your tongue."

About to step up the next stair, Madeline paused and turned around. Her eyes alight with curiosity, she said, "So tell me who it is."

Phoebe shook her head. "I am not one to gossip, Madeline, you know that."

"Oh, don't worry about it. All I have to do is stand outside the door and concentrate. I'm quite sure I shall have his name before too long."

"No, no! You can't do that! I'll tell you." Phoebe looked over the rail, then standing on tiptoe whispered a name to Madeline.

To her immense disappointment, Madeline seemed unimpressed. With a shrug she turned and resumed climbing. "Well, if you don't want to tell me, you don't," she said over her shoulder. "So let us see if we can find Henry."

Without much hope Phoebe trotted behind Madeline to the end of the hall on the third floor where the small cupboard housed the housemaid's supplies. Standing well back, just in case, she watched as Madeline pulled the door open and peered inside.

After a moment Madeline withdrew her head. "I'm sorry to say there's nothing in here but brooms and dusters and what appears to be a handmade sign."

Phoebe wrinkled her brow. "What kind of sign?"

In lieu of an answer, Madeline reached inside and dragged out the square board nailed to a wooden beam. In large scrawling letters the words read, "Danger! Keep off! Wall under repair. Extremely dangerous."

CHAPTER

❈ 11 ❈

"What do you think this is doing here?" Phoebe said, staring at the sign in Madeline's hands.

"I have not the slightest idea." Madeline frowned. "I heard Cecily mention this morning that she had made a sign for the roof garden. This must be the one."

"But what is it doing here in the broom cupboard? I'm sure it can't be of much use there."

"Well, assuming that Henry didn't carry it in here, I have to suppose someone else must have done so."

Phoebe didn't like the look on Madeline's face. She didn't like it at all. "Perhaps Cecily put it there," she suggested knowing how absurd that sounded.

Whatever Madeline had been thinking, she obviously had no intention of sharing it. "Well," she said, as if the whole thing was of no importance, "I think we should just put it back, and I'll mention it to Cecily when I see her."

"Yes, but—"

Madeline looked at her with the potent expression that always made Phoebe feel uncomfortable. "If you want to find Henry before your dancers arrive, perhaps we should go down to the next floor."

Reminded of her own personal crisis, Phoebe nodded vigorously. "Yes, yes. We must hurry. Time is slipping by so fast." She rushed to the top of the stairs, already forgetting about the sign.

Cecily was consumed with fury. After everything that Daphne Morris had told her, it would seem her suspicions had been well founded. Not only had someone chosen her hotel in which to carry out this terrible crime, but also he had tried to make it look like an accident, thereby placing her and the Pennyfoot in jeopardy.

Most important of all, he had deliberately taken another person's life. It surely was the most heinous of crimes. If there was a murderer taking refuge in her hotel, it was up to her to see that he was caught.

Somehow she would see that he paid for what he had done. And if Daphne Morris had information that would help her do that, she must be made to reveal it.

She looked across at the companion sitting stubbornly quiet on her chair. "Tell me," she said, "was Mr. Danbury wearing his uniform when he left the room to search for the dog?" She felt fairly certain he wasn't, but it seemed prudent to confirm it.

The companion seemed startled by the question. "Why, no, he couldn't have been. He didn't have it to wear. When I went down to get the costumes from the steam room, only milady's fancy dress was ready. Mr. Danbury's uniform was still waiting to be pressed."

"And what time was that?"

Daphne Morris frowned. "It would have been about half-past six. I took milady's costume up to the boudoir for her to begin dressing while I took Chan Ying for a walk. When I lost the dog I came back to the room, and Mr. Danbury left to search for him."

She plucked at a fold of her dress, apparently struggling to remember. "It usually takes me fifteen minutes to dress Lady Eleanor's hair, after which I went back to fetch Mr. Danbury's uniform."

"And it was ready then?"

"Yes. It was hanging on the rail outside the steam room with the other costumes." A small sigh escaped. "I came back to the suite with it and hung it in the wardrobe. Lady Eleanor wasn't there. I assumed she'd gone on to the ball. I left right away to help search for the dog. I was worried about him."

"And what time was that?"

"About a quarter to eight."

Cecily leaned forward. "I don't suppose you could think of anyone who might have wanted to meet Lady Eleanor, someone milady would prefer to keep a secret from her husband?"

She could tell the companion was becoming increasingly distressed. Daphne Morris looked left and right as if seeking some escape from the question, and her fingers began twisting at the handkerchief as if any moment she would rip it into tiny pieces.

"It might be easier to tell me about it than P.C. Northcott," Cecily added, hoping to jolt the woman into responding.

Daphne Morris's eyelids fluttered rapidly, then she said in a muffled undertone, "I suppose it could have been Mr. Torrington."

"Keith Torrington?" Cecily echoed in some surprise. She had seen the tall blond man arrive earlier that day. It had been his car she'd watched rumble down the slope to the cove.

Daphne Morris nodded. "Lady Eleanor is most friendly with Mr. Torrington's intended, Lady Luella Maitland. In fact, Lady Eleanor was to have been a member of the wedding party next month." She paused, a shadow crossing her face. "I don't know what Lady Luella is going to say about this, I'm sure. It will be a dreadful shock to her."

"But why would Mr. Torrington and Lady Eleanor wish to meet in secret?" Cecily persisted, feeling she already knew the answer.

She wasn't really surprised when Daphne Morris answered, "Lady Eleanor was very fond of Mr. Torrington. She would have married him many years ago if he had asked her. But Mr. Torrington was not ready to settle for a wife at that time, and so Lady Eleanor married Mr. Danbury. I think she did so to spite Mr. Torrington.''

"And now Mr. Torrington has decided to marry after all?"

"Yes. It distressed Lady Eleanor very much when she discovered that Mr. Torrington was to marry her best friend. She actually introduced them in this very hotel."

"And you think Mr. Torrington wanted to meet Lady Eleanor for a last farewell?"

Daphne Morris's mouth twisted in a wry smile. "No, I don't think that at all. You see, milady discovered today that Mr. Torrington had arranged a rendezvous with another woman this weekend. He is most likely with her this very minute. Lady Eleanor was outraged and threatened to inform Lady Luella of her intended's betrayal. Mr. Danbury himself warned Mr. Torrington of milady's intention."

Cecily's interest sharpened considerably. "How did Mr. Torrington receive that news?"

"I understand he was extremely put out."

"Yes, I imagine he would be." Cecily considered that for a moment. "I wonder, did Lady Eleanor mention the name of the young lady?"

Daphne Morris shook her head. "I don't know if she had knowledge of it." She looked up, straight into Cecily's eyes. "I can't imagine why Mr. Torrington should arrange an illicit rendezvous at this hotel. He knows very well that milady and Mr. Danbury visit here often. It seems very foolish to me to take such a risk."

"It would seem so." Cecily rose, anxious now to investigate further the information she'd received.

Daphne Morris stood, then walked over to the door to open it. "I hope it won't be necessary to repeat everything I've told you."

Following her, Cecily said quietly, "I'll be as discreet as possible."

"Though I suppose it's of no consequence now. In any case, Lady Eleanor will not be able to inform Lady Luella, and Mr. Torrington's secret is safe."

"Yes," Cecily said as she stepped out into the hall. "Those were my thoughts exactly."

The steam room was empty when Cecily arrived there a few minutes later. Whatever clothes had not been picked up by half past eight were delivered to the rooms by the housemaids.

Hoping that the day's list had not yet been destroyed, Cecily hurried over to the blackboards on the wall above the pressing tables.

Obviously Ethel, the laundry maid, had been in a hurry, since the list for that day's orders for cleaning and pressing was still chalked up on the boards.

Fridays were always much busier in the steam room, since many of the guests had their costumes pressed for the ball.

Cecily skimmed down the list, noting that a half-dozen military uniforms had been brought down for pressing. Keith Torrington's name was not among them, however.

When she did discover Torrington's name, she saw that he had sent down a sheikh's costume to be pressed, as well as a Cleopatra ensemble. Interesting, Cecily thought. Considering the need for secrecy, Keith Torrington was remarkably indiscreet.

A thought occurred to her, and she hurried out to the reception desk. If Torrington wanted his visit to remain undetected, he most likely had signed the register under an alias.

The night clerk was apparently resting in the tiny office behind the desk, and Cecily felt no need to disturb him. The register lay on the desk, and she turned it around to read it. What she saw there surprised her a great deal. The signature scrawled across the middle of the page read, Mr. and Mrs. Torrington.

Replacing the register, Cecily frowned. He certainly hadn't gone to any great pains to hide the fact he was accompanied by a woman. Yet Daphne Morris had stated that Mr. Torrington was most put out when Robert Danbury warned him of his wife's intention to inform his bride-to-be of his tryst.

Deciding it was time she had a word with Keith Torrington, Cecily glanced at the grandfather clock in the foyer. She wasn't at all certain as to how she could broach the delicate matter of his companion, but somehow she had to find out if Torrington had sent the note to Lady Eleanor.

While she continued to ponder the problem, she heard her name called. Looking up, she saw Madeline hurrying down the stairs, her pale lilac gown billowing out behind her.

Cecily could tell from the set look on Madeline's face that all was not well. She waited until the other woman reached her before asking, "Have you found Henry?"

"No, Phoebe is still searching for him." Madeline took her arm and drew her into a corner, though there were no ears to overhear their conversation. "I found something else," she said in a dramatic whisper.

"What is it?" Cecily whispered back, without quite knowing why.

"I found a hand-painted sign warning people about the danger to the wall."

Cecily forgot to whisper. "Where is it?"

"On the third floor. It was in the broom cupboard. I was looking for Henry in there, and it fell into my hands." Madeline looked pleased at Cecily's stunned expression. "I thought you'd be surprised."

She leaned forward, dropping her voice to a whisper again. "Who do you think put it there?"

That was something she'd dearly like to know, Cecily thought wryly. She wasn't ready to discuss the matter with Madeline right now, however. Conscious of the woman's sharp gaze, Cecily said casually, "Baxter, I expect. Now that the wall has a huge hole in it, I imagine he decided the sign would be unnecessary and put it away."

"Oh" Madeline said, obviously disappointed. "I thought perhaps there might be dirty deeds afoot."

"Dirty deeds?" She was altogether too quick, Cecily thought, doing her best to seem confused at the thought. The last thing she needed was for rumors to be spread that Lady Eleanor's death might not be an accident.

Though she was very much afraid that once P.C. Northcott arrived and heard what she had to say, he would most likely send for the inspector. There didn't seem to be any way to avoid a full-scale scandal now.

"Well, Cecily," Madeline said, looking up and down the hall to make sure no one could overhear, "it does seem awfully odd that Lady Eleanor would venture near a dangerous spot in the wall, leave alone actually lean against it. But if by some chance the sign weren't there, well that would explain it, wouldn't it?" Madeline lifted a finger and laid it along her cheek. "Now just suppose someone had deliberately hidden the sign, before Lady Eleanor went up there. I have to wonder what that would suggest to you."

Her train of thoughts so closely matched Cecily's own that she became most concerned. "It suggests that you are being even more fanciful than usual," she said, introducing an edge of disapproval into her voice. "I do hope you are not expressing such thoughts to anyone else."

Madeline looked hurt. She wagged a slender finger in Cecily's face. "I warned you this morning," she said, dropping her voice to a husky whisper. "Murderers murder on the night of the full moon."

"I would appreciate it if you'd keep those thoughts to yourself, Madeline. If you have time to spare, perhaps you could help Phoebe with the tableau? I'm afraid this business with Henry has put her all behind."

Madeline sighed. "I was intending to go home. I have nothing but a sausage roll inside my stomach, and it's beginning to make the most dreadful noises. If you insist, however, I will see what I can do to help her."

She turned to go, then apparently changed her mind. "You know," she said, "I do believe Phoebe has found someone of interest in one of your suites."

Surprised, without thinking, Cecily asked, "Who?"

Madeline shrugged. "She wouldn't tell me his name and went to great pains to deny it, but he's the gentleman staying in suite three." She fixed her odd stare on Cecily's face. "I don't suppose you'd know the name of the gentleman occupying suite three?"

It was difficult to keep a blank expression under that intense gaze, but Cecily managed it. "I'm afraid I haven't the slightest idea. Who did Phoebe say it was?"

Madeline told her with a laugh that said she wasn't entirely convinced that Phoebe wasn't telling the truth. "I offered to make up a potion for her, but of course Phoebe would never agree to that." She shook her head with a mournful sigh. "I feel so sorry for the disbelievers. They deny themselves so much, instead of trusting in the spirits."

Cecily had the uneasy feeling that the remark was directed at her as much as Phoebe. Madeline knew full well that Cecily did not share her friend's beliefs in the spiritual world she inhabited for so much of her life.

"Anyway," Madeline added, "I'd better continue the search for Henry. The poor dear must be quite upset by all this trauma. I shall have to whisper in his ear to settle him down again when I find him."

She floated off down the hall, leaving Cecily staring after her, a thoughtful frown on her face.

Actually, the mystery surrounding suite three was the least of her worries, she reminded herself.

It had become increasingly clear that the sooner this little matter of Lady Eleanor's death was cleared up, the better. Far too many people were becoming involved, and it would only be a matter of time before word leaked out that Lady Eleanor had met with a fatal accident.

From then on, speculation would be rife, and the ugly rumors could do more damage than the truth. Though Cecily was very much afraid the truth could be quite devastating, if her hunches proved to be correct.

But that didn't seem to be of primary importance now. She would have to set aside her concerns about the possible damage to the Pennyfoot and worry about it later.

What mattered now was to find the identity of the murderer and bring him to justice. She would not rest until that had been achieved.

There was also another consideration. She had yet to discover the reason why Lady Eleanor had been killed. Since milady was still wearing her jewelry, then robbery could be ruled out. But Madeline's warnings about the full moon still played on Cecily's mind.

There was a slight chance that the killer had not been known to Lady Eleanor, but was simply a deranged person who had chosen his victim at random. If so, it was possible he could feel compelled to claim another victim. That thought chilled her to the bone.

CHAPTER

❈ 12 ❈

Cecily glanced at the clock, wondering how much longer it would take for the constable to arrive. She could hardly send for the inspector, since she had no proof to support her suspicions.

Yet even if P.C. Northcott suspected murder he would not be qualified to conduct the investigation himself. And it could be morning before the inspector might arrive. Cecily was not at all happy about that.

The first thing she must do, she decided, was go to the ballroom and find Keith Torrington. Somehow she must find an excuse to speak with him.

At that moment the main doors opened. Cecily was surprised to see Baxter come through them. His hair looked mussed by the wind, and he wore a harried expression as he strode toward her. He carried a lighted lamp in his hand, and she looked down at it as he reached her.

''Where have you been?'' She couldn't imagine what had taken him outside again so close to eleven o'clock.

He smoothed his hair down with the palm of his hand. It was a gesture she knew well. Baxter always did that when under a certain amount of strain.

''I have been to the courtyard,'' he said, lifting the lamp high in the air in order to turn it out. ''John needed a lamp out there.''

''John is still out there?''

''Yes, madam.''

Cecily frowned. ''What's he doing out there in the dark?''

''He is replacing the torn-up plants. There is also a stain on the bricks he wanted to remove before it became set.''

''I'm not sure that's a terribly good idea, Baxter.''

He looked confused. ''I don't understand what you mean, madam.''

''I mean that John is very likely removing evidence of a crime.'' Glancing around to make sure no one was in earshot, Cecily quickly explained about the note and Madeline's discovery of the sign.

''I think that someone wanted the death of Lady Eleanor, and when he saw the sign warning about the damaged wall, he saw a way to bring his wish about. He removed the sign, then invited her up there. Since she was unaware of the danger, it would have been a simple matter to lure her close to the wall, and at the opportune moment—give her a firm push.''

Baxter's face looked pale in the light from the overhead chandelier. ''I have to admit I have considered the possibility. Now in view of this matter with the message, it does seem a very strong likelihood.'' He shook his head. ''Whoever in this world would want to do such a thing?''

''I don't know.'' Cecily hesitated. ''But I can hazard a guess or two. It seems clear to me that whoever sent that note to Lady Eleanor knows a good deal more about this situation than we do. I think we have to determine who sent the note, then confront that person with the evidence.''

Again Baxter's hand smoothed down his springy dark hair. ''We cannot be certain that whoever wrote the note was responsible for Lady Eleanor's death.''

"True. But it certainly seems suspicious, doesn't it? Lady Eleanor is dressed and ready for the ball, waiting for her husband to return to escort her there. She receives an urgent message, apparently summoning her presence to the roof garden, which she obeys. Minutes later she's lying dead on the courtyard floor. I would say that's extremely suspicious, Baxter."

The lamp rattled in his hand, a sure sign that he was becoming agitated. "I think it would be most unwise to accuse someone of such a dangerous crime without proof. That is something that I must strongly urge you to leave in Inspector Cranshaw's capable hands."

Cecily waved a hand in the air. "Oh, piffle. You worry too much, Bax. I don't intend to go charging up to someone and say, 'Forgive me, but I believe you murdered Lady Eleanor, so what do you have to say about that?'" She shook her head at him. "Please, allow me more credit for my intelligence than that."

He tilted up his chin. "So what do you plan to say, if I might ask?"

She huffed out her breath. "I don't really know, to be honest. But I would dearly love to get my hands on that note. If we were to determine the author, that would certainly tell us who it was who invited Lady Eleanor to the roof garden."

"The note is not in her room?"

"That I don't know either." She shook her head. "I spoke with Robert Danbury, of course, but he could hardly invite me into his suite unchaperoned. You could go there, however, if we could think of some pretext as to why you wished to do so."

She could tell that he wasn't fond of the idea. "There is something we could try first," she added as Baxter rocked back and forth on his heels, yet another sign of his anxiety. "We could search the body, in the chance that Lady Eleanor took the note with her."

Baxter paled even further. "Are you certain you should pursue this course? I would suggest it might be far more prudent to wait until the constable gets here."

"We could do that," Cecily agreed. "But let's suppose that

the constable is convinced there is enough suspicion about the accident to warrant an investigation. What will be his next step?''

''If he suspects foul play, he will most certainly send for the inspector. I doubt very much if he would proceed with his limited experience and authority.''

''Precisely. By the time the inspector arrives, it could well be tomorrow. By then our murderer could have left the hotel, and the trail will be cold. This could drag on for weeks. Months. I don't want this hanging over my head for the next several months. I want this taken care of now.''

''If you are worried about the clientele, madam, I assure you curiosity alone will bring them back down.''

''Perhaps. Once the crime is resolved. How many people do you suppose would care to sleep under this roof, knowing there had been a murder here and the culprit is still free and possibly on the premises? Unless we can prove his identity, it could be anyone. Even one of our own staff.''

Baxter looked shocked. ''Surely not, madam!''

''Well, of course not, but not everyone will be as confident of that as we are. It is essential that we find this criminal and clear the name of everyone here.''

She had presented the strongest argument she could think of, and a valid one, to win his support. If she'd mentioned the possibility of a deranged killer, he might well have locked her in the coal cellar to prevent her from investigating further.

To her relief, he saw her point. ''I agree absolutely, madam. We cannot allow any suspicion to fall on the staff.''

Which included his own name. He hadn't mentioned it, but Cecily knew that was on his mind. ''Good, that's settled then. You'll come with me to search the body?''

Baxter sighed. ''I will search the body myself.''

Very relieved to hear that, Cecily patted him lightly on the arm. ''Then let's get to it right away.'' She started to lead the way down the hall, then paused, looking back at him over her shoulder. ''By the way, there's something I need to ask you.''

''And what is that, madam?''

''What's the name of the gentleman in suite three?''

Looking a little puzzled, Baxter scratched his head. "Suite three? I believe that would be Mr. and Mrs. Shuttlewick."

Turning back to face him, Cecily peered at his face. As usual, she could tell nothing from his expression. "Oh, really? Are you sure that's his name?"

"Quite sure, madam." He frowned. "Is there a problem I am unaware of?"

"No, not at all. I was just curious, that's all. Bax, do you happen to be carrying any cigars with you?"

He rolled his eyes to the ceiling, but nodded his head.

"Good, I really have quite a craving for one." Smiling, she led the way down the hall.

The library door, on Cecily's instructions, had been locked, and she waited for Baxter to produce the key to open it. It was the only room that had escaped the extensive renovations that had altered the appearance of the Pennyfoot so drastically.

The Earl of Saltchester, as Cecily had observed more than once, would be unlikely to recognize his former home now if he were to walk in and see it.

She often wondered what had happened to the family. They had become impoverished shortly before the end of the century. Something to do with bad investments abroad, so Cecily had heard, and the family had been forced to sell the estate.

The earl was a distant cousin of Lord Withersgill, whose stately mansion overlooked the village from its vantage point on the peak of Parson's Hill. Known by the villagers as "Hisself," Lord Withersgill was rarely seen in public. In fact, some of the stories told about him were even stranger than those about Madeline.

Although well aware that speculative gossip was an element of village life, Cecily had no time for it. She contended that such talk caused far more harm than people realized.

In a town the size of Wellercombe, the problem would not be quite so acute. A murder would certainly cause a sensation but would be confined to the people involved. In a village, particularly one as small as Badgers End, one person's disgrace brought disgrace on the entire community.

Until the murderer was uncovered, anyone could fall under

suspicion. Cecily was not about to let that happen to anyone on the staff of the Pennyfoot. Even so, she had to admit to a certain queasiness in her stomach when Baxter made to pull aside the cloth covering the body.

"If you wouldn't mind, I would very much like to have that cigar now," she said, seating herself at the table.

"This is not at all proper, madam."

"Oh, to blazes with what's proper. Who's to see?" She scowled at him. "Bax, you'd be far more entertaining if you were not so deplorably stuffy."

"Yes, madam." Baxter straightened, and pulled the cigars from his pocket. "If I might be permitted to say so, I am astounded that you can sit in front of Master Sinclair's portrait and blow smoke in his face. He would be utterly disgusted."

She took the cigar from him before fixing him with her gaze. "No, you may not be permitted to say so. Really, Baxter, I am getting quite tired of you presuming to tell me what I should or should not do. You are taking James's request far too seriously."

"I am doing my best to follow his instructions."

Cecily sighed. "You might as well accept the fact that times have changed. I'm attempting to change with them."

"I don't see why you should find that necessary, madam."

She looked at him suspiciously. That had sounded remarkably like a compliment, but she could never be sure with Baxter. Nevertheless, she softened her tone.

"I sometimes find these changes a little frightening myself, but at the same time I have to confess to a certain exhilaration. It would have been only a matter of time, I'm quite sure, before I would have questioned James's beliefs."

She glanced up at the portrait before continuing. "It's long past the time for women to have the same freedoms as men. I applaud the suffragettes and their determination for reform. In fact, if it were not for the Pennyfoot, I no doubt should be in London joining them on their marches. I hear there's a massive demonstration planned at Hyde Park next week. I would dearly love to attend."

Baxter's eyebrows rose and fell. "At the risk of incurring your wrath, I fail to see how women can further their cause by setting fire to taxicabs and digging up golf courses. I fear the loss of a woman's femininity is most regretful."

"It depends what you mean by femininity." Cecily accepted the match he offered her, leaning forward to allow him to light her cigar. "If you're referring to the barbaric custom of forcing myself into a murderous contraption of bones and wires," she continued after blowing out a stream of smoke, "which were invented by men, no less, thus disfiguring my spine in order for my body to jut out in front and poke out behind, then good riddance, I say."

Baxter opened his mouth to protest, but she forestalled him. "The Germans have the right idea. Women there go out openly in public without their corsets. Not like we British, who are forced to hide behind doors in order to breathe in a natural fashion."

She had, at least, succeeded in bringing color back to Baxter's cheeks.

"Madam! I beg you—"

Warming to her theme, she refused to be silenced. "If by femininity you mean I should twitter like a demented sparrow, fluttering a fan in front of my face every time a man speaks to me, keeping any intelligent thoughts I might have to myself for fear of offending a gentleman, then I say it is high time."

His face looked as if it were carved from stone. Taking pity on him, she added, "I know you mean well, Baxter. But while I admit I was devastated when James died, and convinced I could not live without him, I'm finding I can manage very well. I miss him, yes, but I find working to keep the Pennyfoot afloat both challenging and interesting."

"I understand that, madam, but—"

"And I understand that it must be difficult for you to have to deal with a woman when you've been used to dealing with a man. But it's time men realized that women are capable of so much more than Society demands of them. We have every right to be treated as intelligent and capable human beings, not as slaves put on this earth to attend to the needs of men. Thanks to the suffragettes and their movement, our time is coming. And it's long overdue."

"Yes, madam."

She could see he remained stubbornly unconvinced, but having had her say, she let the subject drop. "Very well, back to the matter at hand. Let's see if we can find that note."

Without another word he returned to the body and bent over it. When he straightened again, Cecily noted with sympathy the gray pallor to his face.

"There is no note here, madam."

"Are you sure?" Frustrated, she stared across the room at the body, which he'd taken care to cover up again. "I really hoped we'd find it there."

He stood at the end of the table, hands clasped behind his back, rocking back and forth on his heels. "I found only two pockets, both empty, and examined the sleeves."

"I wonder if she carried a handbag?" She looked up at him without much hope. "I don't suppose John found anything while he was cleaning up the courtyard?"

"Not as far as I am aware. I'm quite sure he would have mentioned it had he found anything. He was too worried about his plants to concern himself with anything else. He simply couldn't understand how they came to be uprooted from their beds, plucked as clean as chicken feathers, as he so drolly put it, when it appeared the rocks had not been disturbed by the fall."

"Most likely the bricks from the wall bouncing off the rockery," Cecily said, her mind still contemplating the whereabouts of the note.

"That is possible, I suppose."

She looked up at him, noting how pale his face looked again. "Why don't you sit down, Baxter? You look awful."

"I'll be perfectly all right, madam."

She dropped her chin into her hands. "I think I should speak to Keith Torrington. Daphne Morris has suggested he might have been responsible for sending the note to Lady Eleanor."

Baxter looked surprised. "You surely don't suspect a gentleman such as Mr. Torrington could be involved in this affair?"

She tapped the table with her fingernails, wishing she knew what to think. "According to Miss Morris, he had reason to want Lady Eleanor's silence on a delicate matter. But whether he was prepared to kill for it, that's another thing entirely."

A knock on the door prevented Baxter from answering. Quickly stubbing out the cigar, Cecily called, "Come in."

The door opened, and Ethel slid timidly into the room. "Police Constable Northcott and Dr. McDuff have arrived, madam. They wish to speak with you."

Cecily looked up at Baxter and pulled a face. "Well, it's about time. Now maybe we can get to the bottom of this."

CHAPTER

❊ 13 ❊

Cecily nodded at Ethel, who hovered anxiously in front of the door. "Please show them in," she said, rising slowly to her feet. She waited until the door had closed again, then added urgently to Baxter, "While I'm talking to the constable, go to the Danburys' suite and try to find out what happened to that note."

"I really don't know what I will say to Mr. Danbury that won't arouse his suspicion."

Cecily waved an impatient hand. "Tell him you are trying to confirm Gertie's story for some reason."

"Very well, madam." He hesitated. "I think it would be wise to allow P.C. Northcott to question Mr. Torrington."

Cecily smiled. "Don't worry. I really don't consider Mr. Torrington a murderer. Besides, if I talk to him, it will be in the ballroom. I hardly think he could harm me in front of sixty people and a twelve-piece orchestra."

A loud rap on the door announced the arrival of the constable and the doctor. The door opened, and Ethel announced the names. Two men entered and greeted Baxter, who shook their hands, then excused himself. With a swift, significant glance in Cecily's direction, he disappeared through the door.

"Cecily, my bonnie bairn, how are you?" Dr. McDuff strode forward, hands outstretched. "What have you got yourself into now, for pity's sake?"

The Scottish doctor's brogue had been well diluted by years of living in the south. A man full of tireless energy, his blue eyes were constantly in motion, missing nothing. A small neat beard softened his craggy face with its ferocious eyebrows, and his white hair still sprang thick and wavy on his forehead.

He had brought Cecily and every one of her five brothers kicking and screaming into the world, as he was always telling her. He teased her every time he saw her, reminding her that her cuts and bruises had easily outnumbered those of her brothers.

He had always enjoyed her stubbornness in accepting the fact that as she grew older, Society denied her the freedom to join in her brothers' exploits. "A proper tomboy," he'd always called her.

Now well past seventy, he constantly threatened to retire. Cecily couldn't imagine Badgers End without the familiar wiry figure peddling furiously up Parson's Hill on his bicycle to take care of yet another emergency.

The firm grasp of his hands almost destroyed her composure, and for a ridiculous moment she felt like weeping. She hadn't seen much of Gordon McDuff since James's death. He had been a pillar of strength to her and the boys through the entire nightmare of the funeral, and during the first lonely days when both her sons had left to resume their military duties in the tropics.

"You look a trifle pale, lassie," the doctor said, jutting his eyebrows down over his eyes. "Are you all right then?"

"I am quite well, thank you," she said quickly, "though I would feel a great deal better had this not happened, of course."

P.C. Northcott cleared his throat. He was several inches shorter than the doctor, and his protruding belly straining the buttons of his uniform suggested a fondness for a regular pint or two of ale.

He wore a solemn expression as he greeted Cecily a little gruffly. His ruddy cheeks had been whipped to a healthy glow by the night wind, and his mustache extended on either side of his face. With his police helmet stuck on top of his bushy brown hair, he looked to Cecily a little like an inverted flower vase.

The constable's gaze switched to the mound under the white tablecloth. "This the body then?" he inquired unnecessarily in his deep, ponderous voice.

Cecily nodded. "Would you like me to leave?"

"I think that's wise," Dr. McDuff answered for him. "All this canna be pleasant for you."

"It's most unpleasant for all of us, Doctor," Cecily said. "I am appalled that this could have happened in my hotel."

"Most unfortunate," P.C. Northcott said, pulling back the cloth. He was silent for a long moment, while Cecily averted her gaze, then he murmured, "Yes, well, I'll write this up as an accidental death. No witnesses so it will be just a routine matter."

"I don't think it's routine at all," Cecily said quietly.

The constable looked up, his light brown eyes immediately alert. "You stated that she fell from the roof. You have some doubts about that, Mrs. Sinclair?"

"There are certain incidents that seem a little unusual, yes."

Dr. McDuff looked worried. "What are you saying, Cecily?"

"I'm saying that I believe there is a possibility Lady Eleanor's death was not an accident."

The constable straightened, dropping the cloth back in place, and took out a notebook from his top pocket. From the same pocket he extracted a pencil. With extreme thoroughness, he stuck out his tongue and licked the end of it, then flipped open the pad and began writing something down. "Perhaps you'd care to explain exactly what you mean, Mrs. Sinclair."

Cecily recited everything she knew, while P.C. Northcott

kept an inscrutable expression on his face as he silently scribbled away.

When she was finished, the constable slowly closed his notebook. "I really don't think there is anything to worry about Mrs. Sinclair," he said in a tone that suggested she was making a mountain out of a molehill. "I'm sure most of what you're saying seems suspicious, but there is usually a good explanation for it all. Most people get a little hysterical when there's a death like this. Natural, I suppose."

"I assure you, Constable," Cecily said carefully, "I am not hysterical. And everything I have told you is exactly what happened. I have not made it up."

"Come now, Cecily," Dr. McDuff murmured, coming forward to take her arm, "try not to get upset. You've had a nasty shock and—"

"I am not upset." Cecily firmly removed her arm from his grasp. "I am merely trying to get to the bottom of some rather suspicious circumstances."

P.C. Northcott cleared his throat. "Rest assured, madam, I shall report this to my superior, Inspector Cranshaw. Won't be able to reach him until the morning, of course. We'll see what he has to say then."

"Very well." There was little else she could do at this point, in any case, Cecily thought.

The constable tucked his notebook in his pocket. "Now, while the good doctor is conducting his examination, perhaps you would show me where the body was found?"

"I'll take you there." Cecily walked over to the door. Not that it would help much, she thought, since John had cleaned up the area. "Baxter should be back any minute. He had an errand to take care of. We'll stop by the kitchen and collect a lamp, if you'll come this way?"

She led the way down the hall in silence, wondering how Baxter was getting on upstairs with Robert Danbury.

Baxter had worked for James Sinclair ever since he had bought the Pennyfoot Hotel five years earlier. Still suffering from the effects of the illness that had laid him low in the tropics, Major Sinclair had relied on his staff a great deal at first as he struggled to renovate the neglected mansion and establish the small but elegant hotel.

There had been two or three potential scandals, all of which had been successfully concealed from the public. But never, until now, had there been anything as drastic as murder. Baxter hoped fervently that there never would be again. That was, of course, if Lady Eleanor had indeed been murdered. And Baxter had to admit, there seemed little doubt that circumstances pointed in that direction.

He waited for some time before Robert Danbury answered his knock. The new widower looked extremely irritated to find Baxter standing there.

"What now?" he demanded. "Can't I be left in peace?"

"I do most humbly beg your pardon, sir," Baxter said with a slight, stiff-backed bow, "but I wonder if I might have a word with you?"

"What about? Has the constable arrived yet?"

"Yes, he has, Mr. Danbury. I'm sure he will be up to speak with you presently. But this matter is quite urgent, and I'd like to get it settled. I wonder if I might step inside for a moment?"

Robert Danbury looked about to refuse, then stood back. "Oh, very well. But please make it quick."

Baxter stepped through the open door and looked around. His gaze skimmed over the writing table and the inlaid table in front of the fireplace. The note could be anywhere.

"What is happening downstairs?" Robert Danbury demanded. "I hope they are not disturbing my wife's body."

"As little as possible, I am sure," Baxter said soothingly. "As I'm sure you are aware, in a matter of a death, we are compelled to send for a doctor. He is downstairs with the constable."

Baxter caught sight of something in the grate and edged closer. "I assume you will want to make your own arrangements as to transportation to London for burial?"

"Yes, yes, of course." Danbury ran his middle finger across his eyebrow. He looked distracted, as well he might, Baxter thought, having just lost a wife.

He cleared his throat. "Begging your pardon, sir, but I wonder if you might help me in a little matter. One of our maids claimed to have brought a message to Lady Eleanor shortly before her death. Sometimes the maids make up these excuses to gain a little extra free time. I am anxious to confirm that she was speaking the truth. Perhaps you could vouch that she did indeed deliver a note?"

It sounded weak, Baxter had to admit, but it was all he could think of on such short notice.

Danbury frowned. "Note? I know nothing of any message. I have seen no note."

"I see, sir." Baxter moved closer to the fireplace and ran his finger along the mantelpiece, as if checking for dust. "Perhaps Lady Eleanor might have received a note in your absence. Could I trouble you to look around, in case she might have left it somewhere?"

A noticeable edge lined Danbury's voice. "Is this intrusion really necessary at a time like this? I tell you, I have seen no note. I have been wandering around the suite for nearly an hour waiting for that damned policeman. I'm quite sure I would have seen a note had there been one. Now, if you'll please excuse me?"

Baxter dipped his head. "Please forgive me, I am most sorry to have bothered you. Perhaps we can clear this matter up tomorrow, when you've rested."

Robert Danbury nodded, though his eyes were still narrowed in suspicion. "I hope the constable won't make it too long, though I have no idea how I can help him, since I know nothing myself."

"I think I can arrange that, sir." Baxter bowed his head in a curt nod and left the room. He was anxious to find Cecily. He had something most interesting to tell her.

"I know we're going to get into trouble," Ethel whispered nervously as she and Gertie crept up the stairs to the second landing. "I don't know why I let you talk me into this."

Gertie was a little worried, too, though she wasn't about to admit it. A bet was a bet and she wasn't about to give up the chance to win one, even if the stakes weren't worth the risk. Her honor was on the line. She had to prove Ethel wrong, and she wanted her there when she did it.

She was about to say so when Ethel stopped on the landing, so suddenly that Gertie crashed into her. "What's the bleeding matter with you?" she demanded.

"Shut up!" Ethel's elbow jerked back and gave her a painful prod in her shoulder.

"'Ere, what—"

"Shut *up!*"

This time the urgency in Ethel's fierce whisper made itself known. Gertie's stomach lurched. "What is it?" she whispered, trying to crane past Ethel's bony body to get a glimpse down the hall.

Ethel jabbed a forefinger across her chest to the left. Turning her head, Gertie caught sight of a man's back disappearing through a door, then it gently closed behind him.

"Who was it?" Gertie hissed.

"That Mr. Danbury," Ethel whispered back.

"Oo, the saucy beast. That's not his room." Gertie licked her lips. "I'd give my best Sunday drawers to know what's going on behind that door right now."

Ethel giggled. "You'd probably lose your drawers if you were behind that door with him."

"Yeah." Gertie sighed. "I bet I could show him a thing or two." She started to visualize the experience, then remembered why they were there. Scowling at Ethel's enraptured face, she added impatiently, "Come on, let's get on with it."

Ethel obediently crept around the landing and began climbing again. "I know we shouldn't be doing this. What if someone sees us?"

"Stop whining," Gertie muttered, "and get on up there. And wait until I'm in the right position before you knock on the blinking door."

"What happens if the lady opens the door?"

"Then you'll just have to find an excuse to open the door wider, so as I can see."

"But what if—"

"Sshh!" Gertie hissed. "Just do it, for Christ's sake."

"Why can't you do it?"

Gertie sighed. "Because I'm not the bleeding maid for that room, am I?"

"But they don't know that."

Unable to find another excuse for avoiding the job, Gertie resorted to blackmail. "Either you open that bloody door or the bet's off."

Ethel stopped dead. "Okay, let's call it off. It ain't worth tuppence anyway."

Encouraged by this lack of conviction on Ethel's part, Gertie grew reckless. "All right let's make it sixpence."

Wavering, Ethel thought about it. "Only if you do the knocking," she said finally.

Gertie did not like that. "What if he's in bed?" she demanded. "He ain't going to be too pleased if I knock him up."

"He ain't going to be any happier if I do it," Ethel said, looking stubborn.

Gertie could see her money and her honor slipping away. She couldn't let that happen, especially since Ethel now seemed most reluctant to go ahead with the scheme. To Gertie that pointed to the fact that Ethel was not as sure about who she'd seen as she liked to make out.

Making up her mind, she said offhandedly, "Oh, all right. If you're too bloody scared to do it, I'll have to."

Ethel smiled in relief. "Go on then. Let's get it over with. I want to go to bed."

Her heart beginning to thump, Gertie crept up the last of the stairs to the landing. Signaling to Ethel to hide behind a potted plant, she slowly stepped forward until she had reached the door of suite three.

Taking a deep breath, she lifted her hand and rapped on the door with her knuckles.

Nothing happened.

When she couldn't hold her breath any longer, she let it out and rapped again. Still the door remained stubbornly closed. Sighing, she turned away. She had taken one step when the door flew open.

Unnerved, she shot a quick glance at the bulky figure of the man who filled the doorway. Shock took her breath away.

"Yes? What is it? What do you want?" a deep voice demanded.

From down the hall came a faint squeak of fright.

The man peered down the hall, then glared back at Gertie. "Well? Speak up, girl. What do you want?"

Gertie got her breath back. "Bloody 'ell," she said and, lifting up the hem of her skirt, fled back to the landing. She hit the stairs running, with a whimpering Ethel behind her, and didn't stop until she reached the bottom.

Phoebe opened the door of the dressing room and was greeted by a babble of chatter and squeals of laughter. Standing around in various stages of undress, the performers were watching a lithe young thing dressed in frilly drawers and chemise, who was executing an outrageous dance, writhing and undulating like some cheap music hall harlot.

The performance was far more lewd than the tasteful steps the dancers had rehearsed under Phoebe's supervision earlier that week. Horrified, Phoebe loudly clapped her hands. "Stop that! Stop it at once! What do you think you are doing?"

The dancers were making far too much noise for Phoebe to make herself heard. Thoroughly irate now, she charged into the room. "Stop it, I say! This is a respectable hotel. You are behaving like whores."

Unfortunately, at the first sight of her, the girls had immediately fallen silent. The last word of her sentence rang down the hall with quite splendid resonance.

Someone giggled, and mortified, Phoebe silenced her with a glare. "Well," she said, bristling with indignation to cover her embarrassment, "I certainly hope you use a great deal more decorum in your performance on stage tonight. Rest assured, if I see one single hip wriggling in an area it's not supposed to be, you will forfeit your pay. I hope I make myself clear?"

The girls nodded earnestly, and she relaxed. This was what she got for hiring cheap labor, she told herself. Now if she'd been allowed to hire professionals from Wellercombe . . .

Sighing, she straightened her hat with both hands. "Good. Now, you all know your places once you get on stage, I trust?" Several heads nodded, but Phoebe was not one to take chances. "Is there anyone here who doesn't know?"

Still reluctant to take the silence as assurance that everyone was thoroughly rehearsed, Phoebe rapidly went over the instructions one last time.

"At the opening bars Dora and Belinda will lead the procession slowly." She paused, then repeated for emphasis, "S-l-o-w-l-y, carrying the pedestal onto the stage, and will then place it in the center. Marion will follow them in with the rest of the dancers."

She rested her gaze on the anxious face of the girl in front of her. "You will no doubt be relieved to hear, Marion, that Henry's basket will be empty. The python will not be appearing tonight after all."

Several audible sighs greeted that remark. Maybe it was just as well, Phoebe reflected. With such unpredictable temperaments as these girls, it might have been tempting fate to trust them with a snake in their midst. Things did have a way of working out for the best after all. And she would simply worry about finding Henry after the ball had ended.

Feeling better than she had all evening, Phoebe completed her instructions with more confidence. "You will hold your positions until the orchestra finishes. And remember," she warned, "I don't want to see anyone so much as breathe." She swept her gaze across the faces, daring them to protest. "Is that quite clear?"

"Yes, Mrs. Carter-Holmes," the voices chanted in unison.

"Very well. I will leave you to finish getting dressed." She cast her eyes over the scanty costumes and hoped no one would take offense. In keeping with the theme, the girls wore baggy harem trousers in sky-blue muslin covered in glittering silver sequins.

They also wore mauve chiffon blouses and silver-fringed bolero jackets. Silver sandals and white veils completed the ensemble, which looked most authentic, she thought. Although no actual flesh was bared, the costumes were bound to cause a stir.

Phoebe had a moment's doubt when she wondered if she should have forgone the dancing and stuck to the tableau alone. But she had to get them on stage somehow, and the opportunity to do some choreography was just too challenging to miss.

Deciding she was probably worrying about nothing, Phoebe

issued a last order to the girls to make haste and stop wasting time with idle chatter, then she left them alone.

It was too bad about Henry, she thought, as she hurried down the hall to the kitchen in the hopes of a quick cup of tea before the performance. But it seemed that it would be a pretty tableau, even if it wasn't quite the spectacular event she'd envisioned.

As for Mr. Sims, well, she would just have to explain things to him. After all, it wasn't her fault some stupid maid didn't know how to mind her own business.

Even so, she couldn't rid herself of an uneasy qualm when she thought about Henry still roaming free around the hotel. She could only hope that he stayed where he was, until Mr. Sims arrived to hunt him down. One accident was quite enough. They certainly didn't need another.

CHAPTER

❈ 14 ❈

John was nowhere to be seen when Cecily and P.C. Northcott reached the courtyard. "He must have gone home," she said, lifting her lamp higher in order to see into the shadowed corners. "He usually leaves much earlier than this, in any case."

"Well, 'tain't no matter. I'll catch him in the morning, if the inspector wants to talk to him."

Cecily nodded. Pointing toward the rockery, she said, "That's where Phoebe and John found Lady Eleanor."

The constable raised his lamp and walked forward to take a look. "A pity you moved the body. Can't tell much once the body's been moved."

"I'm sorry, but it didn't seem right to leave her lying out here in the rain."

The constable nodded. "Ay, that's true enough. Well, can't be helped in any case." He swung the lamp over the rocks, allowing the light to fall on the damp surface. "Can't tell much in this light." He looked up to where the gap in the wall was barely visible against the night sky. "She fell from up there, you say?"

"Yes." Cecily shivered, trying not to think about the unfamiliar view of the lights on Parson's Hill. "I can take you up there, if you like?"

"I think it might as well wait 'til morning. If the inspector wants to inspect the premises hisself, he'll find it a good deal easier to see what he's doing in the daylight."

"Does that mean you won't be questioning the guests tonight?"

P.C. Northcott violently shook his head. "No, no. That wouldn't do at all. Can't disturb the likes of *them* this time of night, can we?"

She would have thought that even the elite upper crust were beyond immunity from the law, Cecily thought wryly. She said nothing, however. She knew well the futility of arguing with the likes of Stan Northcott.

"I think I'll be off, then," he said, brushing his hands one at a time on his hips, as if he'd actually been digging in the dirt. "I'll let Inspector Cranshaw decide if he needs to question anyone in the morning."

Still Cecily didn't answer. She hadn't mentioned Keith Torrington's possible involvement in all this, nor did she want to, until she'd had a word with him. And she fully intended to speak with him. Even if the constable seemed convinced it was an accident.

Dr. McDuff was waiting to leave when she returned to the foyer with P.C. Northcott. He handed the constable the forms he'd filled out, saying, "Not much to report. Death due to a violent blow to the head. Details are all in there." He looked over at Cecily with warm sympathy in his eyes. "You going to be all right, lassie?"

She smiled at him and held out her hands. "I'll be fine, Gordon. Thank you."

He grasped her hands and peered intensely into her face for a moment, then, apparently satisfied, he nodded. "Take care of yourself, now."

She bade them both good night, and watched them ride off together in the trap that had brought the policeman from Wellercombe.

Turning back into the foyer, she saw Colonel Fortescue, whose ruddy face broke into a wide grin when he caught sight of her.

"I say, madam," he said, earnestly blinking at her, "you haven't seen a python slithering about these halls by any chance, what?"

In all the distress over Lady Eleanor, Cecily had almost forgotten about Henry. Wondering how the colonel could have found out about him, she said, "No, I haven't. Are you missing one?"

"No, not me, not me. The little lady who's in charge of the dancing girls. Mrs. Carter-Hobbs."

"Holmes. She told you she'd lost a snake?"

"Asked me to help find it." The colonel's eyelids flapped up and down in agitation. "Can't find the blessed thing anywhere. And it must be getting near the time for the tableau. Don't want to miss that, you know. All those flimsy veils and everything, what, what?"

"Oh, absolutely, Colonel. It would be a great shame indeed if you were to miss such a spectacle."

"Yes, well, that's what I thought. Would you tell the dear lady I did my best? Mission failed, I'm afraid. Dashed nuisance. Dreadful sorry and all that."

Cecily smiled. "Don't worry, Colonel, I'll be sure to tell her. By the way, did you ever find your pith helmet?"

"What? Oh, that. Dashed strange that was. Found it right where I'd left it. Hanging right there on the hallstand. Old eyesight must be going, what?"

He peered shortsightedly down the hall. "Used to have eyes like a hawk. Now I can't even see the blessed clock from here. I say, what is the time, old bean?"

"It's a half hour before midnight." Cecily glanced at his waistcoat pocket. "You don't have your watch?"

The colonel blinked at her. "Watch? Never carry one, madam. Don't care for the pesky things. Not since the army days. Everything had to be done by the blasted clock. Dashed tiresome. Always going wrong, anyway. Bad habit, that is, keep looking at a watch. Days go by fast enough without watching them tick away, what, what?''

''They do indeed, Colonel,'' Cecily agreed. She distinctly remember Mrs. Chubb saying that Gertie had helped the colonel look for his watch. It would seem that someone was not telling the truth.

Knowing Gertie's reputation for inventing stories when it suited her, Cecily added casually, ''One of the maids mentioned that you asked her to help you find your watch earlier this evening. Were you perhaps looking for something else?''

''Maid? What maid is that?'' The colonel looked genuinely confused. ''Don't remember talking to anyone like that, old bean. Don't remember that at all.''

''Don't worry, I'm sure she got you mixed up with someone else.''

The colonel nodded, blinking anxiously. ''Yes, must have. Know the old brain isn't what it used to be, but I'm quite sure I'd remember if I chatted to a maid. Haven't done that in quite a while. Always so busy, you know.'' He gave her a smart salute, then wandered off mumbling to himself.

Thoughtfully Cecily watched him go. The colonel was a little eccentric, true, but not senile. And he seemed quite sure he hadn't talked to Gertie. So if the housemaid wasn't helping him find his watch at half-past seven that evening, then where had she been all that time?

The sweet sound of violins drifted down the hall from the ballroom, disturbing her thoughts. Making up her mind, Cecily headed for the steps leading to the balcony. If nothing else, she wanted to see if Keith Torrington was dancing with the mysterious Cleopatra.

The singing strains of violins, echoed by the deeper voice of the cello and the rippling chords of a harp, filled the sumptuous room. The lush sound soared up into the vaulted ceiling and along the sweeping balconies as Cecily stepped through the balcony door.

Below her, couples twirled gracefully across the sprung parquet floor, gliding in and out of thick marble pillars, while golden cherubs smiled down from the perches high above the dancers' heads.

From her vantage point she looked down on the sea of swirling masked faces. They appeared to be floating in an ocean of delicate pastel satin and taffeta, sparkling sequins and fluttering creamy chiffons. The scene shifted and changed in a kaleidoscope of muted colors, guided by the magnificent music of the orchestra.

A scene like this never failed to move her. She and James had loved to dance. Her body still knew the safe, warm feeling that had crept over her every time he'd taken her in his strong arms and whirled her around the ballroom, her feet barely touching the floor as they skimmed together as light as butterflies on the surface of Deep Willow Pond.

A slight movement farther down the balcony caught her eye, banishing her bittersweet memories. A tall sheikh, resplendent in white robes, hovered over a petite Cleopatra in a shimmering golden gown.

Cecily watched Keith Torrington, for it had to be him, exchange a word or two with the woman. This didn't seem the appropriate time to speak with him, and she was about to turn discreetly away when the woman moved quickly toward the door, no doubt in search of the ladies' lavatory.

The sheikh watched her go, then dug inside his robes for a moment before withdrawing a pack of cigarettes. Taking the chance offered her, Cecily hurried forward.

As she paused in front of him, Keith Torrington returned the pack inside the flowing folds without taking a cigarette. In deference to her, he would wait now until he was alone again. His gray eyes questioned her from behind his mask as he waited for her to speak.

"I'm sorry to intrude upon your evening, Mr. Torrington," Cecily said quickly, "but I have a little matter I need cleared up."

If he was surprised that she'd recognized him, he gave no sign. "How might I be of help?" he asked, giving her a half smile.

Cecily hoped that he hadn't as yet heard the news of Lady Eleanor's death. Taking the plunge, she said, "It has come to my notice that one of the maids was supposed to deliver a message from you to Lady Eleanor early this evening. Unfortunately the maid mislaid the note, and has just now confessed. Since Lady Eleanor did not receive your message, I thought you should be made aware of it.''

A long pause followed while Cecily waited, holding her breath.

''I'm afraid I don't understand. I sent no message to Lady Eleanor. I have no wish to speak with that lady at all. Your maid must have mistaken me for someone else.''

Cecily made a great display of appearing flustered. ''Oh, my, I am so sorry. I really don't know how such a mistake could have happened. I was led to believe that you were anxious to speak with Lady Eleanor on a matter concerning your coming wedding.''

She saw his jaw tighten below the mask. ''Mrs. Sinclair, I don't know who could have given you this information, but I assure you, my wife and I have no wish to discuss our wedding with Lady Eleanor.''

Cecily felt her mouth drop open. ''I beg your pardon? Your . . . wife?''

Again he paused, then answered, ''Lady Luella Maitland and I were married quietly this morning. We eloped in order to escape the intolerable preparations for an extravaganza neither of us wanted. We chose this hotel because this was where we were first introduced—by Lady Eleanor, as it happens.''

He seemed to draw himself up, looking somewhat like an avenging angel in his white-and-gold-trimmed robe. ''We did not expect the Danburys to be here, and if Lady Eleanor is offended because she was not informed of our plans I am sorry. You have my permission to tell her so. You may also tell her that we do not wish to discuss this matter with her and would appreciate some privacy.''

''I am so sorry. Please excuse the misunderstanding.'' Cecily gave him an apologetic smile. ''I can assure you, you have nothing to worry about from Lady Eleanor.''

She left him and hurried back through the balcony door without waiting for his answer. Sooner or later he would hear the news, but she sincerely hoped it would be morning before it reached his ears. She saw no reason to spoil his wedding night unnecessarily.

She met Baxter on the way back to the kitchens. He seemed a trifle agitated, but Gertie blundered through the kitchen door as he opened his mouth to speak, and whatever he was going to say was cut off.

"Oh, madam," Gertie said, tugging a pink knitted shawl around her shoulders, "I was just on me way out. Thought I'd get a breath of fresh air before I go to me room. Hope it's stopped blinking raining."

"I believe it has." Cecily glanced up at Baxter. "Would you wait for me in the library, please, Baxter? I want a word with Gertie first."

Baxter looked disappointed, but nodded and melted away down the hall.

Gertie looked alarmed as she backed into the kitchen. "Nothing wrong, I hope, mum?"

"I hope not, Gertie." A quick glance around assured Cecily the kitchens were empty. Aware that the housemaid knew of Lady Eleanor's accident, she decided to waste no more time.

"Gertie, at half-past seven this evening you took the note up to Lady Eleanor. Is that right?"

Gertie nodded, looking scared.

"You returned to the sitting room at a minute or two past eight o'clock."

"Yes, mum."

"And where were you during that half hour?"

Gertie's bold dark eyes darted from left to right. "I was helping the colonel look for his watch, mum."

"The colonel doesn't have a watch, Gertie. He hasn't carried one since he retired from the army."

For a moment it seemed as if Gertie would brazen it out, then her face crumbled as tears sprang to her eyes. "I'm sorry, madam, really I am. It was Ian, see. I bumped into him on the way back, and he pushed me into the blinking broom cupboard."

Cecily's back stiffened with surprise. "Why didn't you tell Mrs. Chubb that?"

Gertie swiped at her nose with the back of her hand. "I

didn't want to get him into trouble, mum. See, Ian's sweet on me, and he was just being playful, like. It wasn't all his fault, you see . . ." She drew a shuddering breath. "I bet Mrs. Chubb's going to be right mad at me, ain't she?"

"I shouldn't be at all surprised." Cecily shook her head. "I'm not sure how you will explain the fact that it took you thirty minutes to get out of the cupboard, but I suggest you try. First thing in the morning."

"Yes, mum." Gertie sniffed. "Can I go now?"

"Yes, you may. And stay away from the broom cupboards."

"Yes, mum."

Cecily hadn't intended bringing up the subject, so she was surprised when she heard herself say, "Oh, there is something else. Mrs. Chubb tells me Ethel told you she recognized the gentleman in suite three?"

Gertie looked uncomfortable. "Yes, mum, she did."

"Do you think she was telling the truth?"

"Oh, yes, mum, I know she was."

She sounded so certain, Cecily sharpened her gaze. "How do you know, Gertie?"

"Saw him with me own blinking eyes, didn't I, mum. There weren't no mistake. I'd know him anywhere, I would. It was him all right."

Baxter, Cecily thought grimly, had a lot of explaining to do.

Gertie was halfway out the door when she thought of something else. "One moment, Gertie. In which broom cupboard were you?"

She looked puzzled but answered, "The one on the third floor, mum."

"Did you happen to see a sign in there?" Cecily held her hand up to her forehead, her palm horizontal to the floor. "About this tall and this wide?"

Gertie's eyes widened. "No, mum. There weren't nothing like that when I was in there. There was only one broom and some dusters and a dustpan. There wouldn't have been no bleeding room for anything else . . ." Her face blushed scarlet, and she swallowed.

Cecily fought the impulse to smile. "Thank you, Gertie. You may go."

The door closed quickly behind the mortified girl, and Cecily's amusement faded. Whoever had hidden that sign in the broom closet must have done so after Lady Eleanor had fallen to her death.

So where had it been while the murder was taking place? It didn't make sense. She shook her head in bewilderment. Nothing about this entire matter made sense. Anxious now to hear what Baxter had to tell her, Cecily left the kitchen and hurried back to the library.

She paused for a moment in front of the door, steeling herself to enter. The presence of Lady Eleanor's body was most chilling. She wished she could have suggested Baxter meet her in her suite. But that would be far too scandalous for him to contemplate.

He stood by the window, looking out at the dark night when she walked into the room. He turned to face her, looking inordinately pleased with himself.

"What is it?" Cecily demanded. "You've discovered something."

"Robert Danbury denies having seen a note. He says he knows nothing about a message for his wife." Baxter clasped his hands behind his back, a smug expression on his face.

Cecily eyed him with suspicion. "But?"

"I scrutinized the room, just to make sure."

"And?"

"I saw nothing lying about on the furniture, so I moved over to the fireplace to take a look there."

"It was on the mantelpiece?" Cecily asked impatiently. Baxter's habit of dragging everything out for effect was beginning to irritate her.

"No, madam. It was not on the mantelpiece."

"So what, then?"

"I saw something in the grate."

Cecily gritted her teeth. "What did you see, Baxter?"

"Ashes, madam."

"Ashes?"

"Ashes."

She caught her breath. "The note. He burned it?"

Baxter's smile was pure satisfaction. "I couldn't be certain, of course. I tried to get rid of him for a moment so that I could take a closer scrutiny, but he wouldn't budge. One corner of the paper had escaped the flames, however, and I could see enough to ascertain that it was hotel stationery.''

Cecily frowned. ''That doesn't mean it's the note. Either Mr. Danbury or Lady Eleanor could have written anything on a piece of stationery and discarded it.''

''Then why take the trouble to burn it?''

She stared at him. ''Yes,'' she said slowly. ''Why indeed?''

CHAPTER

❈ 15 ❈

"I would suggest that Mr. Danbury delivered the note to Gertie, who took it to Lady Eleanor," Baxter said, a trifle pompously. "She must have left it in the room when she kept the appointment, whereon Mr. Danbury found it, and destroyed it so that his handwriting on it could not be recognized."

When she continued to stare at him in silence, he looked disappointed. "The revelation does not appear to excite you."

She moved over to a chair and sat down. "Baxter, I just don't feel that Robert Danbury killed his wife. For one thing, how could he have possibly done all that in such a short time?"

"All what, madam?"

"Well, listen to this. Robert Danbury leaves the room at fifteen minutes to seven. You see him go through the foyer to the gardens about that time, am I right?"

Baxter nodded. "That's correct."

"He then slips back into the hotel and waits for his costume to be hung on the rack, changes into it, presumably in order to mask his face, and gives Gertie the note at half past seven. He then would have to change out of his costume again, since Miss Morris collected it just a few minutes later, then dash up to the roof garden and wait for Lady Eleanor, who did not leave the room presumably until a quarter to eight."

She paused for breath. "He then pushes her over the wall, hides the sign, races back down the stairs and out into the gardens, to stroll back at ten minutes to eight, seemingly in full command of his breath, which is when I saw him."

Baxter nodded. "Very athletic, madam."

"And seemingly invisible, Baxter." She paused, remembering something. "Though I suppose that would explain the overturned plant pot at the end of the hall. He must have knocked it over in his mad dash for the stairs. I suppose we shall have to inform P.C. Northcott when he arrives back tomorrow morning."

Baxter looked surprised. "He has left already?"

"Yes. I do believe he thought I was making all this up. He certainly didn't seem too concerned by anything I said." Cecily pinched her nostrils with her fingers. She was beginning to develop a headache.

Realizing she still hadn't eaten, she decided to remedy that as soon as possible. "He's decided to wait until tomorrow and report to Inspector Cranshaw. Then it will be up to him whether or not he wants to conduct an investigation."

Baxter sniffed. "I was reasonably certain he wouldn't have the courage to begin on his own. I doubt very much if Northcott would be anxious to open up an inquiry. He is not dealing with villagers in this case, he's dealing with some prominent members of Society. He has only our conjecture to go on, nothing more. If we proved to be wrong in our suspicions, it could prove most embarrassing to Northcott if he were to question the innocence of our guests."

Cecily raised an eyebrow. "You don't care for the constable, do you, Baxter?"

His gaze shifted away from her. "Not particularly, madam."

"Any particular reason?"

"None that I care to discuss." He glanced back at her. "I

can assure you I have nothing to hide that could be construed as illegal or immoral, madam, if that's what you are thinking.''

Cecily raised her hand to her throat. "Why, Baxter, perish the thought. It never for one moment crossed my mind that you could be anything but the epitome of perfection.''

He frowned. "You are making fun of me.''

She studied him for a long moment. "Have you ever thought about growing a mustache, Baxter?''

To her amusement, his cheeks flamed. "No, madam,'' he said stiffly.

"Well, perhaps you should. It would make you look most distinguished.'' She rose and crossed the room to the door. As he came forward to open it for her, she added, "I am going to look in on Phoebe's tableau, then I'll get something to eat. After that, I plan to retire for the night.''

"Yes, madam.''

For a moment her eyes strayed to the still form beneath the white cloth. She hadn't cared for Lady Eleanor, but how sad to think of that poor woman, her life snatched away from her far too soon, lying on a cold, hard floor all alone throughout the night.

She had much to be thankful for, Cecily reminded herself. She looked back at her manager. "Good night, Baxter.''

"Good night, madam.'' He opened the door, and she passed through, smiling at his still-flushed face.

Cecily was about to start down the hall to the ballroom when she heard her name being called urgently from the stairs. Looking back, she saw Daphne Morris clinging to the banisters, her face a stone mask. She beckoned with her hand, a furtive gesture that immediately alerted Cecily.

Hurrying over to the woman, she wondered if Miss Morris had decided to tell her she knew about the message after all. In spite of everything, she had a great deal of trouble believing it could have been Robert Danbury.

Pausing at the foot of the stairs, she looked up at the companion. Something else dreadful must have happened, Cecily thought in alarm. Daphne Morris's face was flushed, her eyes red and swollen.

"I have something of the utmost importance to tell the constable," she said, her voice low and trembling. "Can you tell me where to find him?"

"I'm afraid P.C. Northcott has left for the night. But he'll be back in the morning." Cecily stepped up one stair, bringing her closer to the quivering woman. "Is there something I can help you with?"

Miss Morris hesitated, then gave a quick nod of her head. "I should like to speak to you in private. Could I ask you to come to my room?"

Following Daphne Morris up the stairs to the second floor, Cecily couldn't imagine what had happened to cause the younger woman such distress. In spite of the tragedy, she had seemed quite composed earlier on.

She waited while Miss Morris opened the door and invited her inside the room. Taking a chair, she waited for the companion to sit, but apparently Daphne Morris was much too agitated to sit down. Instead she strode back and forth across the carpet, hugging her body as if she were cold.

Cecily thought of the cigars tucked away in her bureau drawer upstairs and wished she could have one. "What is the problem, Miss Morris?" she inquired. "You appear to be quite upset."

"And so I am." Daphne Morris halted, her arms folded across her small breasts. "Mrs. Sinclair, I have reason to believe that Lady Eleanor's death was not an accident."

Cecily arranged her features in a look of surprise. "What makes you think that, Miss Morris?"

"I believe she was murdered."

"You must have a reason for such a strong accusation."

"Yes, of course I do." Daphne Morris seemed to have trouble swallowing, since she made one or two attempts before going on. "I believe Lady Eleanor was murdered by her husband."

Cecily blinked. "I must say I am shocked to hear you say that. Can you tell me why you believe such a thing?"

Miss Morris turned swiftly away, as if overcome by emotion. When she turned back, she appeared to have herself under control again. "I have had reason of late to suspect Mr.

Danbury of taking a lover. I'm afraid that was confirmed not ten minutes ago. I was on my way to his room to ask if he wanted me to take care of Chan Ying for the night. I thought it might be distressing for him to have such a vivid reminder of his dear wife.''

She paused, her throat working, and Cecily waited, wondering what was coming next.

''I had just reached the landing,'' Daphne Morris continued, ''when the door of his room opened. A young lady appeared in the doorway.'' She swallowed, then went on. ''Not wishing to intrude, I stayed back in the shadows. I was surprised, of course, but thought it might be one of Lady Eleanor's acquaintances, wishing to console Mr. Danbury. I couldn't see too clearly from where I stood.''

She drew the back of her hand across her eyes, as if she could banish the memory. ''When she turned in the light, Mrs. Sinclair, I saw she was a young girl, a complete stranger. And then . . . and then . . .''

''Yes?'' Cecily leaned forward, to catch the whisper.

''He bent his head and . . . kissed her.''

Cecily straightened. ''I see.''

''Can you imagine?'' Daphne's hand fluttered aimlessly in the air. ''His wife lying dead downstairs, not yet cold, and he doesn't have the decency to wait until she's buried, much less mourned.''

Cecily looked at her gravely. ''I admit that appears to be dishonorable behavior, but I really don't think you can assume anything from a simple kiss. It could quite well be as you first surmised, a genuine act of consolation, nothing more.''

Miss Morris shook her head impatiently. ''I can assure you, Mrs. Sinclair, it was not that kind of a kiss. Besides, there is more. In the light from the room I saw it quite clearly, pinned to her collar at her throat.''

''You saw what, Miss Morris?''

''I saw Lady Eleanor's brooch. The one that she had mislaid and accused the maid of stealing. Mr. Danbury must have given it to his lover.''

Cecily had to admit that certainly would seem to clarify

things. "Even so, I don't understand why that should lead you to believe that Mr. Danbury murdered his wife."

"Don't you see?" The younger woman whipped around, her gown floating about her ankles, and began her restless pacing again. "He killed her for her money, of course. If he'd divorced her, she would have made quite sure he never saw a penny of her wealth."

She paused in front of Cecily, breathing very fast. "Robert Danbury was terrified of being poor again. He had a most unfortunate upbringing and was a struggling accountant when Lady Eleanor married him. That's why he married her in the first place. For her money. He was never in love with her."

She bent down until her face was close to Cecily's. "He would never have divorced her," she whispered, as if afraid of being overheard.

"Really," Cecily exclaimed, a little surprised.

"Oh, yes. And I know how he did it. He obviously was the one who sent that note to her. He must have changed into his uniform before I collected it, and he gave the note to the maid to take to Lady Eleanor. He most likely used the supply room next door to the steam room. It would have taken him only a moment or two."

Cecily looked at her, thoughtfully nodding her head. "That would be possible, I suppose." She could plainly see that the younger woman's distress was quite real. And far more gut-wrenching than it had been earlier.

Daphne Morris straightened, tears standing at the corners of her eyes. "If he wanted this other woman permanently in his life, it was the only way. With his wife dead, Mr. Danbury inherits all the money."

She whirled away to resume her pacing once more. "How could he do this to that poor, poor woman? After everything she's done for him. It is despicable." She paused, staring at Cecily across the room with eyes that now glittered with anger. "He must be made to pay, Mrs. Sinclair. We must see that he does. Or that poor, dear woman will never rest easy in her grave."

Cecily rose, conscious of a dull pain increasing in her temples. "I can see you are quite upset," she said kindly. "I suggest you get some rest. There is nothing we can do until the morning, but if you wish to speak with P.C. Northcott when he arrives, I'll arrange it.''

Daphne nodded. ''Thank you, Mrs. Sinclair. I would be most obliged. I do not relish the idea, I can assure you. I am still badly shocked by all of this. But I must tell the constable what I know and bring milady's murderer to justice.''

''I agree, Miss Morris,'' Cecily said quietly. ''I most heartily agree.''

She stood for some time outside Daphne Morris's room after the door had closed behind her. Then, frowning, she made her way down the stairs.

''Come, come, girls,'' Phoebe called out, clapping her hands. ''Places, everybody.'' She shook her head in despair as the girls shuffled awkwardly into position. Dora and Belinda had quite a problem with the pedestal, which really wasn't that heavy.

Phoebe watched them struggle with it, reflecting that young girls of today didn't know what it was to expend their energy. Not like in her day, on hands and knees, black leading the grate or scrubbing doorsteps. Whatever would they do if they were forced to work like that for a living, she'd like to know?

Just when she was about to explode with frustration, they finally got it hoisted onto their shoulders. Marion took up her position behind them, hiding giggles behind her hand.

Phoebe took one last look at the costumes. Isabelle, in her role of the sultan, looked magnificent. Phoebe was most pleased with her choice. Most pleased.

She'd intended to hire a male dancer for the part, but the weight might have been a shade too much for the slender dancers bearing the sedan chair. She'd hired a girl instead and stuck a false mustache under her nose.

It worked very well, Phoebe thought with pleasure. Very well indeed. From the dance floor it would be impossible to tell the sultan was female. Even close up, it was difficult to tell the difference.

Satisfied that she had done her very best, and with a pang of regret for the absent Henry, Phoebe opened the door leading

onto the ballroom. It really was too bad, she thought, looking
out at the orchestra members. They had gone to great pains to
learn Henry's special music. It would have been magnificent to
see him swaying back and forth to it. All that effort for nothing.

"Now remember," she cautioned the dancers, "do not lift
the sedan until your hear the opening bars of the snake-
charming music. There will be a slight pause after the first
piece, when the dancers get into position around the pedestal.
Then, you make your grand entrance. I will be watching from
the floor, so once you are in position, I don't want to see the
flutter of an eyelid."

Isabelle muttered something under her breath that Phoebe
didn't catch, but by then the orchestra, having spied the open
door, had begun a rather stilted version of "Song of the
Sands."

"Go on! Go on!" Phoebe urged as masked heads turned
toward the door in expectation.

Dora and Belinda writhed up onto the stage, almost dropping
the pedestal in their attempt to wriggle their anatomies as much
as possible, to the obvious delight of the crowd watching from
the floor.

Phoebe closed her eyes in despair, then hurried out to the
front of the stage to enjoy her masterpiece.

The orchestra struggled valiantly with the unfamiliar music.
Cecily, watching from the balcony, had to admit the tempo left
much to be desired.

The dancers looked as if they were having trouble keeping in
step, thwarted not only by the unwieldy pedestal they carried
but also by the rapid pace of the conductor's baton.

The piece finally came to an end, probably a lot faster than
Phoebe had intended, and the dancers arranged themselves into
beguiling positions to await the entrance of the sultan.

A roll of drums proved to be rather effective as through the
door came the richly ornate sedan chair bearing its regal
passenger. Brilliant jewels flashed and sparkled in the sultan's
white turban. Beneath it a pale face stared straight ahead
without expression as the procession advanced slowly toward
the stage to an accompaniment of even stranger-sounding
music.

Cecily had to admire the way the girls handled the chair up the steps, even if the sultan did grab the sides of it in alarm at the steep angle. Considering the weight of the "man" they carried, as well as the chair, they were doing very well, she thought.

The ensemble reached the top of the steps, and the sultan settled into a more comfortable position. The violins, led by the flutes, wailed their oddly tuneless melody, and once more the chair moved forward.

Cecily, watching in some concern as to how the girls would lower their cumbersome burden, saw a slight movement behind the resplendent figure seated on the bright red satin cushions.

Then, like the Loch Ness monster emerging from the lake, Henry's ugly head appeared and rose majestically above the sultan's head, swaying ecstatically to the music.

CHAPTER 16

Stunned silence from the floor greeted the spectacle, then a slight smattering of applause broke out, with a ripple of murmured admiration.

The sultan, having apparently caught the appreciative stares of the audience, tilted his head back to see what had caused the excitement. Henry, oblivious to all this, continued to sway to the music.

A shrill scream rang out, and it was a moment or two before Cecily realized it had come from the terrified passenger on the sedan. The bearers, startled by the noise, clumsily and very hurriedly, lowered the chair. Before it had hit the floor, the sultan sprang from his perch. In his haste, he became tangled in his robes.

Seconds later the turban fell to the ground, revealing long, golden tresses. Which was not entirely a surprise, since by then the sultan, in his frantic effort to escape, had dragged off his robes, revealing in no uncertain terms that ''he'' was in fact a female.

Leaping off the stage, the screaming girl headed for the door, followed by the rest of the dancers. Panic, swift and infectious, swept through the crowd on the floor. Women fainted dramatically right and left, some of them caught in the arms of their gallant escorts, some not so lucky.

Cecily caught sight of Phoebe, her face hidden by her hat, which had been tilted forward in the melee, attempting to fight her way through the now uncontrollable mob who were frantically seeking escape.

The sultan reached the door and plunged through it. Concerned about Henry's reaction to all this uproar, Cecily glanced back at the stage.

The orchestra had abandoned their positions, leaving a very confused python, which had slithered out of the chair, swaying uncertainly in the middle of the floorboards.

Cecily was most likely the only person to see Madeline climb the steps to the stage, approach the huge snake, and lift it in her arms, then with it wrapped contentedly around her neck, she walked back to the steps and disappeared down them.

Her head throbbing painfully, Cecily stared down at the pandemonium below her. If Madeline's spirits were indeed responsible for this catastrophe, then they had surpassed themselves. Thank God it was midnight. The day was finally over.

''Mercy me,'' Mrs. Chubb exclaimed after Cecily had recounted the entire nightmare. ''I heard the rumpus going on, but took no notice. It usually gets noisy in the ballroom when they take them masks off.''

''Not quite that noisy,'' Cecily said grimly. Seated at the kitchen table, she leaned an elbow on it and rubbed at her forehead with her thumb and forefinger.

Mrs. Chubb peered down at her. ''Got a bad headache then, madam?''

Cecily nodded. ''I really should eat something before I go to bed. With everything that's happened tonight, I had to forgo dinner.''

Mrs. Chubb tutted. "Just you sit there, and I'll get something right away. I'll give you one of my powders, too. Does wonders for headaches, it does. My Fred used to swear by them. 'Specially toward the end, when his headaches got so bad."

Cecily watched her bustle over to the huge cupboards and pull one open. Mrs. Chubb had been a widow almost four years. Cecily wondered how long it had taken the housekeeper before she could fall asleep at night without aching over the empty space next to her.

Nights were the worst. The thought of climbing into that cold empty bed and the long hours when she couldn't sleep weighed heavily on her. She pushed the melancholy thoughts away and managed a smile as Mrs. Chubb put a half-empty bottle of brandy down in front of her.

"Put some of that in your tea, mum. It will do you the world of good. Gave some to Phoebe, I did. She brightened up in no time."

"I can imagine." Cecily looked at the label. "I see Michel's taste is still impeccable."

Mrs. Chubb lifted her hands and let them drop. "Well, you know the chef, mum. Nothing but the best. 'Specially when it's going in his stomach."

"Well, I really can't say too much. He is an excellent chef, and they are so very difficult to come by in this part of the country."

"If you want my opinion, everything is difficult to come by in this part of the country." Mrs. Chubb lifted a finger. "Which reminds me, I have to get another jar of my special piccalilli out. I'll slice up some pressed beef while I'm in the larder, and how would you like a nice hunk off of Michel's cottage loaf?"

Cecily nodded wearily. "That sounds delightful, Mrs. Chubb. "Perhaps some Gorgonzola and an apple?"

"Coming right up." She hurried out of the kitchen, a roly-poly figure in her white pinafore apron and dark brown dress.

When the housekeeper returned and put the loaded plate down in front of her, Cecily was quite sure she'd never seen anything quite so appetizing. She tucked in right away, with Mrs. Chubb hovering anxiously nearby.

"So what happened to the snake, then?" Mrs. Chubb asked when she sat back with a satisfied sigh. "Did Madeline get it back into its basket? How did it get into the chair, anyway?"

Cecily patted her mouth with her serviette. "As far as we can make out, when Ethel disturbed him, Henry decided to take a look around. Phoebe had all the props for the tableau stored right there next to him. He must have found the sedan chair, decided to adopt it as his new home, and promptly went back to sleep. Phoebe was so certain he'd escaped through the door, she didn't think to look anywhere else."

Mrs. Chubb shook her head. "Poor Phoebe. She was in such a state. I bet she's glad it's all over."

"I'm sure she is. Mr. Sims arrived a little while ago to take charge of Henry. It was not a tearful farewell, I can assure you."

"I'll just bet it wasn't." The housekeeper opened a cupboard and took out a glass. "I'll fix that powder for you now, mum. You'll sleep like a baby tonight."

Sleep like a baby, Cecily's thoughts echoed. That would be nice. That would be very nice indeed.

She slept fairly well after all and woke to a bright, sunlit morning. Standing at the open window, she could look down on the tennis courts and the rock pool beyond. Dew sparkled on the sunlit grass, and sparrows twittered loudly as they perched on the heads of the strange-looking topiary animals John had carved out of the yew.

Listening to the steady *thwock* of a tennis ball against a racquet in the clear, cool morning air, Cecily found it hard to believe the events of yesterday had actually happened. She wondered how Robert Danbury felt, waking up to his first morning without his wife.

She hoped he did have someone with whom he could seek consolation. There were times when she would dearly love to have such a person herself.

A light tap on her door interrupted her thoughts. She crossed the room in bare feet to answer it, smiling when Gertie greeted her carrying a jug of hot water.

Although two bathrooms had been installed in the Pennyfoot, Cecily still preferred to wash in her room when the hotel was full. "Thank you, Gertie, I'll take it," she said, reaching for the jug.

"Morning, madam. Mr. Baxter said to tell you they've arrived to take the body to the station."

"Already?"

"Yes, mum. Ian says they want to catch the first train to London."

"I see. Is Mr. Danbury leaving with it?"

"No, mum. He's staying behind to pack the trunks. I heard Mr. Baxter tell Mrs. Chubb as how Mr. Danbury don't want to travel with his wife's body."

Cecily nodded. "Well, thank you, Gertie. I might have a visit from Inspector Cranshaw and P.C. Northcott this morning. Please inform me if they arrive. I'll be going down for breakfast in half an hour."

"Yes, mum." Gertie closed the door.

Cecily carried the jug over to the washstand and poured water into the bowl. She wondered if the inspector would be a little more astute than his constable—though she would not look forward to a meeting with Inspector Cranshaw. Unlike Stan Northcott, his superior was a tall, unsmiling, aloof man who had a way of staring into people's faces as if he could read their minds.

She had met him only twice, and both times he had made her feel guilty about nothing, which was ridiculous, of course. Cecily splashed the lukewarm water on her face. She just hoped that he could make more sense out of this whole situation than she could.

On the one hand, it seemed as if Robert Danbury had to be the obvious suspect for murder. He had much to gain from his wife's death, and his marriage was far from perfect, according to Daphne Morris.

Cecily rolled soap between her palms, then massaged her face. But if he was guilty, she would dearly love to know how he had accomplished it. Something wasn't quite right about the scenario she had envisioned. And she just wished she knew what it was.

Patting her face dry, she decided there wasn't much more she could do. Baxter would no doubt be relieved to hear her say that. From now on, the investigation was in Inspector Cranshaw's hands. Still feeling decidedly uneasy, she finished dressing.

Much to Cecily's satisfaction, the inspector arrived with P.C. Northcott shortly after breakfast. Apparently he'd decided to take her seriously, although the meeting went no better than she had envisioned. At her request, Baxter remained in the library with her during the interview.

Determined to deliver her account as fairly as possible, Cecily was most careful what she told Inspector Cranshaw. She recounted her conversations, as close as she could remember, with Robert Danbury, and those with Daphne Morris. She omitted her conversation with Keith Torrington, since she saw no purpose in bringing up the subject.

During her entire speech, Inspector Cranshaw said nothing, nor could she tell from his expression what was in his mind. She was surprised he didn't take notes, though P.C. Northcott scribbled in his notebook from time to time.

"I admit, a good deal of it doesn't appear to make sense," she said when she had finished recounting everything that had happened. "The business with the note, for instance. It would seem—"

"Mrs. Sinclair," the inspector interrupted. "I thank you for your interest, but I must caution you about interfering in business that does not concern you. Our job is difficult enough and would be made considerably easier were it not for well-meaning members of the public taking it upon themselves to meddle in our affairs."

Resentment burned in Cecily's cheeks. "I was doing my best to help. Since I was on the premises and you were not, it seemed at the very least advisable to ask a few preliminary questions of my guests."

"That was Police Constable Northcott's duty, madam," the inspector said in a patronizing tone. "Unfortunately the constable obviously did not feel he had sufficient reason to question anyone. We shall remedy that this morning and draw our own conclusions, however. I should appreciate it if you will allow us to do that without interruption?''

If he meant for her to stay out of his way, Cecily thought, she would be most happy to oblige. ''Certainly,'' she said, keeping her voice cool. ''I am anxious to have this matter cleared up as soon as possible. Obviously this terrible tragedy does not speak well for the Pennyfoot.''

The inspector nodded. ''I can understand your concern, madam. If this should prove to be a simple accident after all, you could well be held responsible, in view of the condition of the safety wall.''

Something in his voice annoyed her. ''That is not why I have drawn your attention to my suspicions,'' she said, resisting the urge to hit him. ''I certainly hope you will uncover the solution before too long.'' She stood, indicating the end of the conversation.

The inspector rose smartly, with the constable lagging a little behind him. ''Thank you for your assistance in this matter, madam. I assure you, we will do everything in our power to determine the truth.''

Relieved that the ordeal was over, she could afford to be gracious. ''Please let me know if there is anything else I can help you with,'' she said. ''I am sure Mr. Baxter will be most happy to assist you should you need to speak with any of my staff.''

The policemen left, and she sank onto a chair, thankful to have the meeting over with.

''Are you feeling all right, madam?'' Baxter inquired after the door had closed behind the two men. ''If I might comment, you sounded a trifle irritated.''

''Insufferable man. He as good as called me a meddlesome old woman.''

''I think he was merely concerned for your well-being, madam.''

''Well-being be blowed. I might have known you'd take his side. Typical masculine attitude.''

She looked up to find his face stiff and expressionless. ''Oh, all right, I apologize. Forgive me, I didn't sleep well last night.''

"Nor I, madam. It made me most uncomfortable to know that we very likely have a murderer in our midst."

She didn't see the point in telling him that wasn't the reason she had lost sleep. "I'm glad you, at least, share my beliefs. That makes me feel a little better."

"I don't think the inspector disbelieves you, madam. I think he simply wants to conduct his investigation in his own way."

Cecily sighed. "Maybe you're right. Perhaps I am being a little unreasonable. All this unpleasantness has made me very tense. I think I shall go out into the gardens and get some fresh air and sunshine. Perhaps it will help to clear my head and wake me up."

"I think that is an excellent idea." He moved to the door and opened it. "I will be sure to inform you when the police are finished with their investigation."

"Please do." She allowed her gaze to wander into the corner where Lady Eleanor had lain all night. "I must say, I feel much more comfortable in this room now that they've taken the body away."

"Yes, madam. I sent Ian out late last night with a message to the undertakers to be here as early as possible."

Cecily nodded. "One of these days I'll be able to afford to have a telephone installed. James always argued with me over it, saying he didn't consider it a necessity. But there are definite times, Baxter, when it would come in most useful."

"Perhaps all changes are not necessarily detrimental."

Cecily smiled. "I have hopes for you yet, Baxter."

"Thank you, madam."

She could have sworn she saw a smile forming as she swept past him.

Wandering around the gardens some time later, Cecily saw John Thimble weeding the flower beds by the rock pool. Kneeling among the hollyhocks and Canterbury bells, he started when she spoke to him. He scrambled to his feet, pulled off his cap, and stood twisting it in his hands.

Cecily looked at the carefully tended beds and smiled. "It all looks so beautiful, John. I don't know how you manage it all single-handedly. I admire your dedication to it. This is such a large place to take care of."

"Yes, mum."

She shaded her eyes with her hand to look across the croquet lawn. "I hope the rockery didn't suffer too much from yesterday's awful tragedy?"

"No, mum. I took care of it all right."

"Thank you, John. I appreciate you working so late last night."

"Yes, mum. I be happy to do it, I'm sure." He followed her gaze, deep furrows carved in his tanned forehead. "Can't think how them plants came to be torn up like that, though. Mystery to me, that were."

"Well, as long as they didn't suffer because of it. That's the important thing, isn't it?"

He looked at her, his face breaking into a smile at her understanding. "It is indeed, mum. It is indeed."

She smiled back. "Oh, as long as I'm here, I just thought I'd mention that the grass on the tennis courts looks a little long."

"Yes, mum. I'll be getting to that this evening. I were going to do it yesterday evening, but then that Mrs. Carter-Holmes had me looking for that there snake." He blinked anxiously in the sunlight. "Did they find the snake, mum?"

Cecily nodded. "Henry is safe and sound, back with his trainer. Mr. Sims collected him very late last night."

"That be a big relief, mum. Wouldn't want no snake wandering around these gardens, here. Could do no end of damage to plants, that he could."

Not to mention people, Cecily thought, amused by the groundskeeper's priorities. "Oh, indeed, John," she said gravely. "He could indeed."

Gazing past her, John pointed his cap at a spot behind her. "Here come Mr. Baxter, mum. Looks like he might be looking for you."

Cecily spun around and saw Baxter hurrying across the lawn. Even from that distance she could tell by his gait and the set of his shoulders that he had something urgent to tell her.

Excusing herself, she walked to meet the manager, wondering what new catastrophe was about to erupt.

Baxter slowed his pace when he saw her coming, smoothing his hair back with his hand as she approached.

"What is it?" she demanded as he got within earshot.

"The police have finished with their investigation," he said, a trifle out of breath.

Cecily peered at his face. "And?"

"I thought you should know right away, madam. They have taken Robert Danbury in for questioning for the murder of his wife."

CHAPTER

❊ 17 ❊

"I still find it so hard to believe," Cecily said as she walked back across the still-damp grass with Baxter.

"I don't know why, madam. I thought it was a foregone conclusion. You suspected Lady Eleanor had been murdered, and everything pointed to him as the culprit. Who else had reason to kill her?"

Cecily shrugged. "You are right, of course. And yet my instincts tell me he wasn't responsible." She looked up at him. "Did he confess, do you know?"

"No, madam. He didn't. He emphatically denied it, of course. According to Northcott, he looked quite threatening when the inspector arrested him."

"P.C. Northcott told you?" Cecily inquired innocently.

Baxter gave her a disparaging glance. "The constable can be most informative at times. He enjoys being in a position of importance, and was anxious to talk about the case."

"Not that you were at all anxious to listen, of course."

"I thought you'd want to know as many details as possible."

"Ah, so you did it for me."

"Yes, madam."

He paused for so long she grew impatient. "So tell me, then," she demanded.

"There isn't much more to tell. From what I understand, Gertie identified Mr. Danbury's uniform as being the one worn by the man who gave her the message last night. She saw that a button was loose, and remembers thinking that it would be another one to add to Mrs. Chubb's button tin."

"Really. How odd."

Baxter looked down at her. "I do not see what is odd about that, madam."

Cecily stepped onto the crazy paving path. "Never mind, Baxter. Was there anything else P.C. Northcott told you?"

"Well, there were the ashes in the fireplace. And I understand a paper knife was found in Mr. Danbury's room badly scratched. The inspector believes it was used to work the bricks loose in the wall. Apparently, upon close inspection, he discovered that the wall had been tampered with."

"Really? Then it wasn't the fault of the storm at all."

"No, madam."

She sighed. "I would so have liked to know how Robert Danbury managed it. That is the real mystery here, Baxter. How did he do it? How did he have the time to do it?"

"He is a young man. Under duress people can do extraordinary things."

They had reached the steps leading up to the main doors, and Cecily mounted them, still brooding over the news. Reaching the top step, she paused. "You know, Baxter, there's something else about this that I don't understand."

He looked down at her, one eyebrow raised in question. "And what is that, madam?"

She hesitated, then shook her head. "No, I need to think about it for a while. In the meantime, I think I should have a word with Daphne Morris. She will have to take care of everything on her own, and I feel I should offer our services should she need them. I presume she's still here?''

"Yes, madam. Miss Morris informed me she would be staying until tomorrow, as originally intended, in order to take care of the packing. Since Mr. Danbury will not be returning to London for now, Miss Morris will have to see that the Danburys' trunks are packed and returned to their home.''

He pulled open the heavy door and held it for her. ''Northcott asked that the suite be locked until he can return to pick up what evidence he needs. He has given Miss Morris permission to pack everything except Danbury's uniform, but he wants no one else in the room until he has cleared it.''

Cecily nodded, only half-listening.

"I pity that poor lady," Baxter said, surprising her. "She will have a difficult time of it, I'm afraid.''

"Yes," Cecily murmured as she stepped into the foyer. "I'm quite sure she will.''

Having found Daphne Morris's room empty later, Cecily went up to the Danburys' suite. When she tapped on the door, Miss Morris opened it with an alacrity that surprised her. The companion's eyes still looked a trifle puffy, as if she had spent a good deal of the night weeping.

Accepting her invitation to enter the suite, Cecily walked in and looked around. An open trunk sat in the middle of the room, half filled with clothes.

Gesturing at it, Miss Morris said wearily, "As you can see, I am packing everything to take back to London.'' She walked over to an armchair and dropped down on it. "I must say," she added, passing a hand across her eyes, "I shall be quite thankful to get back to the city. I really don't think I can manage any more of this dreadful business.''

Cecily took the chair opposite her and leaned forward. "I am sure it must be a great relief to you to know that Mr. Danbury has been taken for questioning.''

Daphne Morris's face hardened. "Well, of course, I did not enjoy seeing him led away in that fashion, but, yes, I do admit to a certain easing of my mind. At the very least, Lady Eleanor will now rest easy in her grave, knowing that justice will be done.''

"And we can all rest easy in this hotel, knowing that the murderer has been apprehended." Cecily paused. "What will you do now, Miss Morris? Have you considered your future? Have you any plans?"

"I have given it a great deal of thought." The other woman sighed. "I will have to begin looking for another position, of course. I am hoping that Lady Eleanor left me a small sum to manage on until I find something."

"I'm sure she must have." Cecily straightened her back. "I am here to tell you, Miss Morris, that if there is anything we can do, please do not hesitate to ask."

Miss Morris nodded. "Thank you, Mrs. Sinclair. You have been most kind. I am indeed grateful."

Cecily rose. "I shall be dining in the dining room this evening, if you would care to join me. There is no reason for you to have dinner alone."

The younger woman gave her a weak smile. "Thank you. I am not interested in food at the present, but if I have found my appetite by tonight, I shall be pleased to join you."

"In that case," Cecily said, moving toward the door, "I shall hope to see you tonight."

Outside in the hall, she paused when Miss Morris said suddenly, "Mrs. Sinclair, there is something you could do for me, if it wouldn't be too much of an imposition."

Looking back at her, Cecily gave her a polite smile. "Of course, Miss Morris. What is it?"

The companion hesitated. "It's Chan Ying. I shall have to find a home for him. He is getting old, and his temperament leaves much to be desired, but I was wondering . . ."

She left the question unfinished, a hopeful expression on her face as she looked at Cecily.

Oh, Lord, Cecily thought. "By all means, Miss Morris. Don't worry, I'm sure I can arrange something."

"Thank you. I would be so grateful." The door closed quietly, and Cecily grimaced. She had nothing against dogs, but that yappy little pest did not belong cooped up in a hotel.

Maybe she could ask Madeline, Cecily thought, as she headed back down the hall. She could add it to her menagerie.

Madeline was in the library when Cecily walked in there later. Her arms full of John's bright red snapdragons, she was replacing the drooping roses, which had lost more petals during the night. To Cecily's relief, she readily agreed to take the Pekingese.

Cecily rescued a pink rosebud and stuck it through a buttonhole in her blouse. "They look nice and bright," she remarked as she watched Madeline's quick, capable hands create design out of disorder.

"Not much smell though," Madeline said, standing back to take a look. "I do like a flower with a heavy perfume. I've been trying to talk John into growing wildflowers. Some of them have the most exquisite fragrance. But you know John, he is so set in his ways."

Cecily smiled. "He has very definite ideas on how to take care of the grounds here. And he does an excellent job. He has practically landscaped the entire area."

"Oh, I'm not saying he doesn't do a good job. I agree, he has a wonderful green thumb. It would be nice if he were just the tiniest bit adventurous, that's all."

The thought of John Thimble being adventurous made Cecily smile. "He is a very quiet man," she murmured. "A very private man."

"That's because he has some deep, dark tragedy in his past. He has buried it away in a place where it can't gnaw at him."

Cecily looked up in surprise. "How do you know that?"

Madeline looked mysterious. "I can sense it. Whenever I am near him. It's like an aura floating around him. Something happened to make him stop living inside. That's why he stays away from people."

She plucked a long stem, heavy with blossom, from the bowl and broke off a piece of it before replacing it. With her head bent to one side, she murmured, "He doesn't like people, you know. Not really. I don't think he trusts them."

Cecily felt uncomfortable, as if they were prying into the man's deepest, most private being. She was about to say so when Madeline added quietly, "We all have them, you know."

Startled, for some reason Cecily felt a chill. "Have what?"

"Secrets. All of us have something hidden away inside of us that we don't wish anyone to know."

Cecily wasn't sure how to respond to that. She was quite relieved when a light tap on the door announced a visitor. The door opened, and Phoebe poked her head around it, bumping her hat as she did so and setting the huge brim askew.

"Oh, there you are, Cecily." Phoebe stepped inside the room and pulled the hat pin out of her hat. "I have the invoice for last night's ball. I couldn't see Mr. Baxter to give it to him, so I'll give it to you." She straightened her hat and stuck the pin back in.

Cecily stretched out her hand. "Thank you, Phoebe, I'll see that he gets it."

Phoebe handed over the slip of paper and shivered. "My, this place still has the feel of death, doesn't it? To think that poor woman lay here all night. I shall never feel the same about this room."

"It doesn't seem possible that someone should be murdered right here in this hotel," Madeline murmured, standing back to admire her handiwork.

Phoebe let out a shriek. "Murdered? Surely not?"

Cecily sighed. "I'm afraid so. It will be common knowledge before too long."

"Oh, dear great good heavens." Phoebe flapped a hand in front of her face. "I think I'm going to faint. I must sit down. What a dreadful thing."

"It's already common knowledge in the hotel," Madeline said, rearranging an errant stem. "Everywhere I went this morning, people were talking about it. Apparently someone saw Robert Danbury being led away by the police, and in a matter of moments just about everyone knew."

Phoebe's eyes grew as round as croquet balls. "Robert Danbury . . . killed his wife?"

"He has been taken in for questioning, yes," Cecily said, a little sharply. "But he has not been charged as yet, as far as we know. Even then, it is up to the courts to prove him guilty, not the likes of us."

Madeline looked at her in surprise. "You talk as if you think the police made a mistake."

Cecily shrugged. "I simply do not believe in condemning a man without knowing the entire story, that is all." In an effort to change the subject, she added, "Baxter assures me that no one was hurt last night, Phoebe. I do trust the dancers are uninjured?"

Phoebe nodded gloomily. "What a disaster. Such an embarrassment. Why I did not look in the chair I really can't imagine. I simply assumed Henry had gone exploring, when all he'd done was find a better place to sleep. The cushions were the same color as his own, so he must have thought they had been provided for him."

She looked across at Madeline. "Are snakes capable of recognizing colors?"

"Not really. But I don't know why you are so concerned. I thought it was quite exciting. All those women swooning into their lovers' arms? It caused the biggest sensation you've achieved so far."

Phoebe groaned. "That kind of sensation I can well do without. That poor girl up on the chair. I am really surprised she didn't break a leg or something." She smoothed a wrinkle out of her glove. "If I had hired a man the way I intended in the first place, none of it would have happened. A man might have received a fright, it is true, but he would never have let out that dreadful caterwauling which set off such a panic among the ladies in the audience."

Madeline smiled. "Just think how much pleasure you gave all those gentlemen. How often do they get the opportunity to watch a delectable young maiden in a state of undress flee across the floor right in front of their very eyes?"

Phoebe tossed her head. "I might have known, Madeline, that you would see the debauched side of things. The poor thing could have been quite badly hurt when the silly girls dropped the chair."

"Well, she wasn't," Cecily said in an attempt to soothe ruffled feathers. "Thank goodness. We had quite enough trauma last night as it was."

"Yes, indeed." Phoebe rose from her chair. "Well, I must

get home. Algie is waiting for me to sew a button on his shirt. I don't think that foolish woman who does for me has ever held a needle and cotton in her life. Every button she sews on comes right off again. I have decided that it would be far more simple if I were to sew them on myself."

She reached the door and looked back. "Oh, Cecily, I have a marvelous idea for the ball next week. A circus theme. I know where I can hire a dancing bear—"

Madeline let out her gurgling laugh and clapped her hands. "Wonderful! I adore the idea. A dancing bear. Will I get a chance to have a turn around the floor with him?"

Cecily frowned. "Perhaps we should wait until the meeting on Monday before we decide," she said to Phoebe. "We'll discuss it then."

Phoebe sighed. "Oh, very well. But I do think it is such a good idea." She closed the door quietly behind her.

Madeline threw her hands up in the air. "She is such a wonderful tonic. I wish she would just learn to relax."

"Well, perhaps you can have a word with the spirits next week," Cecily said, bending her head to sniff the rose in her buttonhole. "Maybe you can ask them to look upon us a little more kindly for Phoebe's next effort."

"It isn't the fault of the spirits, Cecily," Madeline said, walking toward the door. "It takes something special to summon them. What happens after that is out of our control."

She turned and leveled a look at Cecily across the room. "Do not place the blame on the spirits for the failures of human beings. The spirits can only create the frame of mind; it is the body that commits the deed. There has to be an earthly reason for everything, and if things are not what they at first appear to be, it is simply because we have not looked deep enough for the truth."

She paused, then laid a finger on her cheek. "Are you satisfied, Cecily Sinclair, that you have looked deep enough?" She opened the door, then added softly, "I think not."

She closed the door gently, leaving Cecily frowning at the spot where she had stood.

CHAPTER

❁ 18 ❁

Cecily sat for a long time at the table, her gaze on James's portrait. All that talk about spirits and such was pure nonsense, of course. And yet Madeline had an uncanny way of discerning one's thoughts.

It was true, somewhere in the back of her mind Cecily had a strong inkling that she was overlooking something important. Some piece of information that she was aware of, and was not making full use of it.

Yet she had told the inspector everything she knew. If there was something there that could prove useful, surely he would have recognized it.

Perhaps he had. That could be the reason he had felt secure enough in his judgment to arrest Robert Danbury. Because she would certainly not have done so had she been in his place.

Cecily sighed. But then she was relying on instinct as much as solid information. And no matter what evidence had been presented so far, she still couldn't ignore the feeling in her bones that told her something was very wrong.

The timing was so impossible. That was the problem. If she could just work out that particular point, she might be able to feel easier about the situation.

Alone in the quietness of the library, she felt very close to James at that moment. If only he could help her see what it was her mind hid from her. But her thoughts remained as stubbornly unfruitful as ever.

Her gaze fell on the bright red flowers and the glow of them reflected in the polished table. The blurred image reminded her of spilt blood, and she suppressed a tiny shudder.

The inspector had been most annoyed with John for cleaning up the courtyard. She wondered if the groundskeeper had mentioned the torn-up plants. Strange thing, that . . .

Cecily sat up straight, her mind racing. That was it. It was certainly part of it. Her fingers curled into her palm as she thought about it. And the more she thought about it, the more certain she became.

Once more she lifted her gaze to James's likeness on the wall. "Thank you, my love," she whispered. "I should have known you would find a way to help me."

Pushing her chair back, she stood. She had to find Baxter right away. She wanted him to be there when she put her theory to the test. And if she was right, she would know, at last, how Robert Danbury had killed his wife.

Baxter was in the kitchen, speaking heatedly with Michel when she found him. The slender, dark-eyed chef danced up and down in the middle of the stone floor, arms flapping, looking a little like a disjointed marionette at the mercy of his master's strings.

His tall hat bobbed back and forth as his eyes flashed at Baxter. "You want I leave, yes?" Michel's black mustache positively bristled. "I leave now. *Toute suite.*"

Gertie, her arms covered in soap suds, stood at the sink watching with great enjoyment.

At least the chef wasn't drunk, Cecily thought with relief. Michel's French accent tended to disintegrate into London cockney when he'd been at the brandy. It was Baxter's contention that the upredictable chef assumed the pretense of a Frenchman in order to hide his identity, most likely to escape from an irate husband. Michel made no secret of his prowess with women.

Cecily, being more charitable, maintained that the guise was in order to enhance his reputation, either for cooking or enchanting the ladies.

"No, I do not wish you to leave," Baxter said stiffly. "I merely want you to pay attention to what you are doing. I had several complaints this morning about the scrambled eggs not being salted."

"I salt the eggs this morning. I distinctly remember." Spinning on one foot, the chef plucked the wooden condiment shakers from the shelf above the fireplace. "I shake them, so!" He demonstrated, sending a spray of salt and pepper over the grate.

"Blimey," Gertie muttered, "it'll be me who has to clean up that blinking mess."

"What I believe you did," Baxter said in his brittle voice, "is that you took hold of the pepper pot a second time in mistake for the salt."

Michel was momentarily taken aback. Recovering quickly, he fixed Baxter with a lethal stare that dared him to contradict. "So, I try a new recipe," he said with an expansive shrug. "So it not work."

As diplomatic as ever, Baxter accepted this bald-faced lie. "I would suggest that you adhere to the original recipe. It has always been extremely well received up until now. I see no reason to change it."

Appeased, the chef nodded vigorously. "I stick to what is good, no?"

"Precisely." Having settled the matter, Baxter turned to Cecily. "I beg your pardon, madam. Is there something I can do for you?"

"Yes, as a matter of fact there is." She gave him a meaningful look. "I wonder if you can spare me a few minutes?"

"Certainly, madam." Baxter opened the door with a flourish and allowed her to pass through ahead of him.

Out in the hall, she smiled up at him. "Well done, Bax, you handled that admirably."

He tried not to look pleased. "The man is most aggravating, but he is an excellent chef. Sometimes it is necessary to bite one's tongue rather than risk losing such a valuable asset to the hotel."

"My sentiments exactly." Hitching up her skirt, she led the way up the stairs to the foyer.

Once there she was drawn into exchanging greetings with several guests, and more than one asked her about the rumors circulating the hotel about Robert Danbury. Much to her relief, Baxter tactfully fielded the inquiries.

After only a few moments, they were able to make their escape through the main doors.

"Might I ask what you have in mind?" Baxter asked, sounding a little anxious as he followed Cecily down the crazy paving path to the rose garden.

"I want to show you something," she told him. "I think I've discovered how Robert Danbury killed his wife."

"Ah, then you now believe he is guilty?"

"I suppose he must be, if my theory is correct." Even so, she admitted silently, she still retained a niggling doubt that refused to go away.

"And the answer is in the courtyard?"

"Yes, I believe so. I just hope John isn't there, for I'm afraid he will be most unhappy with me for what I'm about to do."

Baxter looked a little alarmed. "I trust you are not planning anything dangerous, madam?"

"No, Baxter, I'm not. But you'll have to keep your patience until we reach there." From across the lawn, laughter mingled with the crack of a croquet mallet against a ball, and in the holly trees the beautiful clear song of a blackbird rang out across the gardens.

The fragrance from the sun-warmed roses filled her with bittersweet longing. James had always loved this time of year. So had she, once. Now it was so hard to look upon the sweet sounds and smells of summer with anything but an ache for all that she had lost.

To her relief John was not in the courtyard when they entered it. Nor were any of the guests, which left her free to carry out her demonstration.

Moving over to the rockery, she pointed at the spot where Lady Eleanor's shattered head had rested. "This is where we assumed milady landed, after her fall from the roof, I believe?"

Baxter nodded slowly. "As clearly as I can remember."

"It must have been a very strong wind, to blow her off course." Cecily looked up at the gap in the broken wall. "At least a good twenty-four inches, wouldn't you say?"

Baxter tilted his head back to take a look. "It is possible she bumped into the wall on the way down, sending her over to the side."

"True. But I don't think so." Hitching her skirt above her ankles, Cecily stepped up onto the rocks.

"Madam, please be careful," Baxter protested, stepping forward as if to detain her.

"Oh, don't worry, Bax, I know what I'm doing."

"Yes, madam. But I would not want to face John's displeasure if you should disturb his plants again."

"I'm afraid I shall have to risk that." Stooping down, Cecily grasped the heavy rock with both hands and tugged. It came up easily, bringing with it the newly planted edelweiss and rock roses.

They clung to the damp surface for a moment, then gravity won, and as she hauled the rock high in the air the fragile plants flew off, and scattered across the smooth brick floor.

Baxter stared at them for a long moment, then as Cecily lowered the rock again he muttered, "Good God in heaven."

Still holding the heavy object she said breathlessly, "Well, Baxter, what do you make of that?"

He looked back up at the wall, then down at her again. "It would appear that Lady Eleanor did not fall from the roof garden after all."

"No," Cecily said, well satisfied with his answer. "She didn't fall. I couldn't imagine how the plants came to be scattered about when the rockery itself hadn't been disturbed.

I started wondering if the rocks had been moved when milady fell, and someone had replaced them before John came on the scene. I wondered if perhaps that's what Robert Danbury had been doing when I saw him return from the gardens.''

"And why would he bother to do that?'' Baxter said, jumping ahead of her as usual.

"Precisely. The only reason he'd have to replace the rock was if he didn't want anyone to know it had been moved in the first place. *Because it was the murder weapon.* As you can see, there are blood stains on it.''

"Yes, indeed,'' Baxter said, frowning as he raised the rock again.

"She was killed right here in the courtyard,'' Cecily said with a note of triumph. "That's how Robert Danbury managed to get up and down the stairs so quickly. He didn't go up them in the first place. The note told Lady Eleanor to meet him here, in the courtyard. He knew it would be deserted at that hour, with everyone preparing for the ball. He waited until she had her back turned on him, then lifted up this rock and brought it down on her head.''

"But the broken bricks from the wall—''

"Were pushed off after he'd killed her, to make it look like she'd fallen. And that's when he hid the sign. I couldn't think why he would hide the sign after she'd died. But he did it to make it look like an accident, of course. It wasn't necessary to remove it beforehand.''

Baxter looked down at the rockery again. "Most ingenious.''

"Yes, indeed.'' Cecily lowered the rock back into place. "There are, however, one or two questions still unanswered.''

"And that is?''

Arms outstretched for balance, Cecily stepped down onto the ground. "I would like to know how he arranged for the dog to escape from Daphne Morris, thereby giving him an alibi and an opportunity to commit the crime.''

Baxter's eyebrows raised. "That is a good question. A very good question.''

"And what do you think might be the answer?''

"It appears that Miss Morris might have had a hand in that.''

"That's the conclusion I came to."

"But it makes no sense. Why would Miss Morris help a man murder his wife, then turn around and accuse him of the crime?"

"Because," Cecily said slowly, "she was in love with him. With Lady Eleanor dead he'd be free to marry her. She said he'd never divorce his wife. He would be left with nothing and he couldn't bear to be poor again. I thought it strange at first that she would know such a personal thing about her employer's husband. But supposing that companion was also his lover?"

"But if she loves him enough to have taken such a terrible risk to help him, why would she then accuse him as the murderer?"

"Because she found out he already had a lover. It would seem that Mr. Robert Danbury used his charm to get Daphne Morris to help rid him of his wife because he was in love with someone else. Once the deed was done, he had no more use for his wife's companion."

"But wouldn't he expect her to denounce him, once she found out?"

"Not if she were likely to be involved. If a man is willing to murder his wife for his own ends, I hardly think he would be gallant enough to keep her name out of it, particularly if she had accused him of the crime."

"But that is precisely what she did."

"Exactly. I think perhaps in the heat of the moment she was distressed enough to throw caution to the wind. I think it likely that she doesn't care what happens to her now that she's lost him, and she just wants revenge."

"That could be. So Robert Danbury underestimated her." Baxter shook his head. "I still find it difficult to believe."

"So would I," Cecily admitted, "if it were not for something else."

"And what is that?"

"The second question. How did Daphne Morris know that the gentleman who handed Gertie the note wore a military uniform? I made no mention of it, yet she suggested to me that Danbury could have changed into his uniform just before he gave the note to the maid. That puzzled me for some time, until I realized she must have been aware of Robert Danbury's plans."

"I see. That would be why she didn't bring the uniform up with Lady Eleanor's costume?"

"Of course. She left it there for Robert Danbury to change into. He had to have a way of hiding his face from Gertie, and the mask was the perfect answer. No one would think it odd for him to wear one with his costume for the ball."

"It all falls neatly into place. I must say, madam, I am impressed with the way you have worked things out. So you will no doubt be contacting Inspector Cranshaw to tell him of your theory?"

"No, I don't think so." Cecily knelt to pick up the bedraggled plants. "I imagine Mr. Danbury will inform the inspector of Miss Morris's involvement, and he will work things out for himself. I intend to do my best to put the matter out of my head. It is over and done with, and I would very much like to forget it as soon as possible."

"I think that is an excellent idea."

"I do think we should replant these poor flowers first. John would be horrified to find them in such a sorry state again."

"I'll do it right away." Baxter stepped up onto the rockery and grasped the misplaced rock in his hands. Carefully balancing it upon another slab close by, he reached out to Cecily to take the plants from her.

"I'm not sure I shall be able to replace them as neatly as John would have it, but with luck they will settle themselves down before he notices."

Cecily smiled. "I would tend to doubt that."

Baxter took a delicate rock rose from her and turned to place it in the gap.

Watching him, she was startled when he uttered a sharp exclamation.

"What is it?" She leaned forward in an attempt to see what he had seen.

Baxter plucked something from the unearthed rocks and held out his hand to her.

Looking down at it, Cecily saw a small round white object lying in his palm.

"What is it?" She took it in her fingers and brushed off the soil clinging to it. "It's a shoe button," she said in surprise.

"Yes, madam. John must have missed it in the darkness when he replanted the plants."

"I wonder where it could have come from?"

"It most likely could have been there for a long time."

"I don't think so, Baxter," Cecily said slowly, turning the white button around in her fingers. "It looks too shiny and new. And certainly a coincidence that it was lying under that very rock, is it not?"

"Perhaps, madam." He held out his hand for the rest of the plants.

She watched him replace them and carefully lay the rock back in place, her mind struggling with this new discovery.

"It might not be the precise job that John would have managed," Baxter said, brushing his hands together, "but it is the best I can do."

"Don't worry," Cecily murmured, "I'm sure they will be just fine."

"Yes, madam." Baxter rose to his feet, slapping at his knees. He glanced at her face as he stepped down from the rockery. "Is something wrong, madam?"

She sighed. "Yes, something is very wrong. I have to think about this, Baxter, but I have a very strong feeling that the pieces don't fall into place after all. I think perhaps my first instincts were true, and Inspector Cranshaw might very well have the wrong man."

CHAPTER

❖ 19 ❖

Cecily spent the next hour in her suite, going over all the possibilities raised by the discovery of the shoe button. Nothing seemed to fit, and again she had the nagging feeling that she had missed something. But try as she might, she could not bring it to the surface.

Finally she decided to go down to the kitchen and get a cup of tea. That would perhaps help to clear the cobwebs from her mind.

Nearing the foot of the stairs, she saw Colonel Fortescue hovering nearby, and was tempted to turn back in order to avoid him. Then she chided herself. He was a paying guest and deserved the same consideration she would afford anyone else. Reluctantly squaring her shoulders, she marched down the stairs to greet him.

"I say, old bean," he said in an exaggerated whisper, "jolly exciting about our visitor, what?"

Cecily shook her head. "I'm sorry, Colonel, I'm afraid I don't understand."

He poked out an elbow to nudge her, thought better of it, and withdrew it again. "You know, the chappie in suite three."

Not again, Cecily thought wearily. She hadn't had time to again corner Baxter over it, but she certainly would at the very first opportunity.

"I'm afraid I don't know who is in suite three," she said firmly. "Now if you'll excuse me . . . ?"

"Ah, but I do. Couldn't believe my eyes at first. I mean, you don't expect to see him in a place like this, what?"

Cecily stiffened. "In a place like what, Colonel?"

"Oh, no offense, m'dear, no offense. Just meant that a big cheese like him is more at home on the continent. Must make you dashed proud, that's all I can say."

"Colonel, I have no idea what you are talking about." To her intense relief, he decided to change the subject.

"Topping show last night, what?" he said, his face lighting up with excitement. "Never saw such a spectacle. Dashed amusing, I thought. Wonderful how they managed all that. Marvelous spot of directing. That Mrs. Carter-Hobbs does a bang-up job, I must say."

She didn't have the heart to explain that the unfortunate episode was totally unrehearsed and quite unexpected. "Thank you, Colonel," she said, smiling graciously. "I'm so glad you enjoyed it."

"Enjoyed it? I haven't had a laugh like that since my adjutant's saddle slipped and left him hanging upside down under the horse's belly. Traveled half a mile before anyone could stop him. Always was dashed incompetent."

Cecily nodded, still smiling. "Well, if you'll excuse me—"

"Couldn't get my breath for laughing when that young woman dashed off the stage. Could've sworn it was a man. Just goes to show, one can never tell nowadays . . ."

He went on talking and blinking, but Cecily wasn't listening. Something he'd said had struck a chord. A very loud chord. She saw again Phoebe's sultan, springing from the sedan chair and shedding her robes in a frantic attempt to escape from poor Henry's benign presence.

So that was how it was done. Of course. How could she possibly have missed it? Nodding and smiling at the colonel, without the slightest idea of what he said, she turned the situation over in her mind.

Again, it was pure conjecture. And yet now she felt certain she had hit on the true answer. But would the inspector listen to her? Most unlikely. He would simply be annoyed with her for meddling, and certainly wouldn't thank her for suggesting he had made a mistake. Even if she showed him the button, she doubted very much if he'd listen to her.

No, she needed proof before she talked to the inspector. And a witness. She hoped Baxter would be willing to go along with whatever scheme she could invent.

The clock struck four times, and the colonel broke off whatever he was saying. "Great Scott! Is that the time? I'm late for my afternoon snifter. Got to stay alert, you know. Never know when the little devils are going to attack."

He threw her a smart salute, somehow managing to poke himself in the eye. Muttering a watery-eyed farewell, he took off at a rapid pace in the direction of the bar.

Cecily watched him go, her brow creased in concentration. There had to be a way, if she could just think of it. Deep in thought, she paid no attention to the voice behind her, until it repeated, "Madam?"

Turning, Cecily smiled down at the housekeeper. "I'm sorry, Mrs. Chubb. I'm afraid I was woolgathering."

"That's all right, madam. You've had a lot on your mind lately, indeed you have. I sent Gertie up to your suite, but she must have just missed you. Got a letter for you, from abroad. She said she pushed it under your door."

"Oh, how nice. It's most likely from one of the boys. I'll look forward to reading it. I was just on my way for a cup of tea. Do you happen to know where Baxter is?"

"I saw him leave a short while ago, mum. I believe he went to fetch the mason to get the wall mended. Said as how it was too dangerous to leave, so he took the trap to get him."

"Never mind. I'll talk to him when I get back." Cecily started toward the steps to the kitchen.

She paused as Mrs. Chubb said, "I hear they arrested Mr. Danbury this morning, mum?"

"They took him in for questioning. I don't think they've arrested him as yet."

"Could've knocked me down with a feather when I heard that. Such a nice, polite man. Doesn't seem possible, does it? I mean, you never know, do you?"

"No," Cecily said slowly, "you never know."

"I mean, you can't tell from looks anymore, can you? Handsome devil. Gertie was right upset about it, I can tell you. Seeing as how it was her what did him in. Would never have known if it hadn't been for that loose button, she wouldn't. I think she wishes now she'd kept her mouth shut. Haunt her for weeks, it will. Be a long time before she can look at that button tin without thinking about it."

Cecily gave the housekeeper a long, thoughtful stare.

"You all right, then, mum?" Mrs. Chubb asked, looking worried.

"Mrs. Chubb, last night when you found that broken jar of pickles—what time was that, do you remember?"

The housekeeper grabbed her chin and frowned. "Well, let me see, it was after Phoebe left in the trap. I'd gone out to see her off. I was a bit worried about her. When I came back, there was the jar on the larder floor. What a mess! Took me ages to clean it up, it did—"

"Yes, I'm sure it did. But what time was that?"

"Must have been near on half-past eight, I suppose." Mrs. Chubb lowered her hand and peered at Cecily. "What's wrong, then?"

"Nothing, Mrs. Chubb," Cecily said brightly. "In fact, I think everything is going to work out just fine. I've changed my mind about that cup of tea. I have something to do. Would you lend me your keys for a little while?"

"Very well, mum." The housekeeper unhooked the ring of keys from her belt and handed them over. "Is there something I can help with, mum?"

"No, thank you. I think I can manage this on my own."

The other woman still looked concerned, and more than a little curious.

Cecily gave her a smile. "If you see Baxter, would you please tell him I'm looking for him?"

"I'll tell him as soon as he gets back, mum."

"Thank you." Feeling quite excited, Cecily mounted the stairs.

Miss Morris was not in her room when she reached the second floor and tapped on the door. Apparently the companion was still packing the trunks in the Danburys' suite. It took Cecily only a moment or two to sort through the keys, fit one in the lock, and slip inside the room.

A few minutes later, outside in the hall again, she quickly locked the door, a satisfied smile on her face. Now all she had to do was put her plan into action.

She quickly climbed the stairs to the third floor and stood in the shadow of the potted plant, prepared for a long wait. Much to her relief, no more than five minutes passed before the door to the Danburys' suite opened. Daphne Morris stepped out, locked the door, and headed for the stairs.

Cecily waited until she was out of sight before choosing a key from the ring and fitting it into the lock. The door opened quietly, and she peeked into the room.

The trunks still sat in the middle of the sitting room, waiting for the footman to collect them in the morning. Cecily stepped inside the room and closed the door.

The lids of both trunks stood open, as if Daphne Morris had forgotten something in the midst of her packing. If so, she could return at any moment.

Hurrying across the thick carpet, Cecily hoped that Danbury's uniform was still hanging in the wardrobe. She wasn't happy about the idea of taking it, but she consoled herself with the thought that she was only "borrowing" it and would have it back before the police constable arrived the next morning.

Holding her breath, she opened the door of the wardrobe, then breathed a sigh of relief. The uniform hung in lonely splendor, looking a little forlorn without the benefit of its owner's broad shoulders.

Cecily carefully lifted it off the bar and rolled it up into a tight bundle. Then she quietly shut the wardrobe door, praying that Miss Morris wouldn't look in there again. It was a chance she'd have to take.

Tucking the uniform beneath her arm, she moved quickly to the door and eased it open. The hall was empty, at least for the moment.

She stepped outside and locked the door behind her. Reaching the landing, she looked over the rails and to her dismay saw Daphne Morris hurrying up the second flight of stairs. There was only one place to hide, and that was the door to the roof garden.

Cecily tucked the bundle she carried under her arm and rushed for the door. Thrusting the curtain aside she grasped the handle and turned it. The door was locked. Baxter must have locked it last night.

Her hand shook as she sorted through the ring of keys. It was too late. She heard Daphne Morris say in a puzzled voice, "Mrs. Sinclair?"

Cecily dropped the bundle to the floor, and pushed it behind the curtain with her foot. Praying the companion hadn't detected the movement, she turned and smiled at her.

"Oh, Miss Morris. I was just about to go up and inspect the damage to the wall. We are hoping to get it repaired shortly, if Baxter can reach the mason."

Daphne Morris's frown faded slowly. "I am sure it must be a great worry for you, to have a gap like that in the wall. So very dangerous."

"Yes, indeed." Cecily drew a breath. "How are you managing with the task of packing? Are you finished with it?"

"More or less. I had left the keys in my room, and had to go back and fetch them. I was just on my way back to lock the trunks. I hope it will not be inconvenient to you if I leave them there until the morning?"

"Not at all. We won't be using the suite until next weekend. Ian will bring the trunks down for you in the morning. You will be catching the midday train?"

Cecily froze as Daphne Morris's gaze dropped to her feet. "Oh, while I think of it," she said quickly, hoping to catch the other woman's attention again, "I plan to be in the dining room at eight o'clock this evening. I do hope you will be able to join me?''

Miss Morris looked up again. ''I would be most pleased to accept. I do not care to eat dinner alone in public.''

''Yes, I feel the same way. Eight o'clock then?''

Miss Morris nodded. ''I will be there.''

Cecily let out her breath. ''Good. Now, is there anything else I can help you with?''

To her immense relief, the companion fitted her key in the lock. ''Thank you, no. It is all done.''

Afraid to move away from the curtain, unless the bundle rolled out, Cecily was forced to wait until Daphne Morris had entered the suite and closed the door behind her.

Without wasting another moment, Cecily grabbed up the bundle and sprinted for the stairs. She didn't breathe again until she was safely inside her suite.

On her way back to return the keys to Mrs. Chubb later, Cecily found Baxter in the foyer, talking to an earnest young man with unruly red hair and a mass of freckles covering his face.

Ben Parkinson's father, Alf, was the local brick mason and apparently had been called away to repair the seawall in Wellercombe, which had been damaged by the recent storm.

Ben, Cecily discovered, had finished his apprenticeship with his father and was now anxious to prove his mettle. ''This is my first job, Mrs. Sinclair,'' he told her with an air of importance she found utterly disarming. ''You can rest assured by the time I'm finished with that there wall, you won't be able to tell it were ever damaged, that's my promise.''

''Well, thank you Ben. I am sure we can count on you.''

Behind him Baxter's expression said he sincerely doubted it. ''Come with me, then, young man,'' he commanded in a tone that put a look of apprehension on the young man's face. ''Let us see if your work is as inspiring as your promise.''

''I need to speak with you when you come down,'' Cecily said. ''I will wait for you in the rose garden.''

He looked surprised but gave her a brief nod before leading the impatient young man up the stairs to the roof.

Outside the hotel, the air had cooled considerably. A stiff evening breeze rustled the leaves in the row of plane trees bordering the croquet lawn.

Cecily glanced up at the white clouds scurrying across the sky and hoped it wasn't blowing up for yet another storm. She particularly hoped that it would not rain that night. Her plan depended on moonlight to a certain degree.

She stood watching a lively croquet game between several of the guests until the game was finally won, and the players departed in order to get dressed for dinner.

Wandering into the rose garden, she hoped that Ben would make short work of the repairs on the wall. She had missed her daily excursion to her retreat that day. It was like missing a rendezvous with James.

She sat down on a garden bench, alone with her thoughts. The perfume of the lush blooms once more brought the familiar ache to her heart. Leaning forward, she snapped off a tender rosebud and held it under her nose.

Every evening throughout the summer she had broken off a rosebud and tucked it in James's lapel. She smiled and drew in the sweet, nostalgic fragrance. It had been six months. Six interminably long months. Yet she had survived. Perhaps it was time, at last, to let go.

Not of the memories—she would always have those to keep close to her heart—but the pain, the longing, the senseless wising that things could be as they once were. They would never be that way again. She had to go on. James would want her to go on.

A tear slid down her cheek and fell onto the white petals. It glistened there for a moment, and was then absorbed. It was time.

Taking the rosebud she wore from her buttonhole, she held the two together and knelt in front of the bush. Gently she lay the delicate flowers side by side and scooped a handful of earth over them to cover them up. "Good-bye, James," she whispered. "Good-bye, my love."

She was still kneeling there when Baxter came upon her several minutes later. "A weed," she explained when she saw him looking down at her, his face full of concern. "John must have missed it. So unlike him."

She scrambled to her feet and gave Baxter a bright smile. "Now, how is that young man doing with my wall?"

To her relief, Baxter chose to ignore any signs of her heartache that might still be visible.

"He seems confident enough. We can only hope his competence matches his enthusiasm. I left him up there to take measurements and calculate his supplies."

"When will he be able to make the repairs?"

"He has promised first thing Monday morning."

"Ah, that will be wonderful. I will feel so much better when that has been taken care of."

"Yes, madam." He hesitated, apparently unsure of what was expected of him. "You mentioned wanting to speak to me about something."

"Ah, yes, Baxter, come and sit down here, and I'll explain." It amused her that he put as much space between them as the bench allowed. "But before I get into that, there's a little matter I'm very anxious to clear up."

Baxter looked wary. "Yes, madam?"

"The gentleman in suite three. I would very much like to know who he is."

As far as she could tell, his puzzlement was quite genuine when he said, "Mr. Shuttlewick. I believe I already told you that."

Cecily nodded. "Well, yes, you did, Baxter. But I have heard comments from several people that lead me to believe that Mr. Shuttlewick is not his real name."

Bewilderment settled over his features. "It is not? Then what is his name?"

Cecily repeated what she had heard.

"I hardly think so, madam," Baxter said sharply. "I took the booking myself."

"And have you seen the gentleman in question?"

"Well, no, but—"

"Then how do you know it isn't him?"

"I think I would certainly have been informed if it were."

"Not necessarily. Not if he booked under an assumed name."

Baxter stared at her for several seconds, then shook his head impatiently. "This is ridiculous. It is most likely someone who resembles him, that is all."

That was Cecily's theory, too, though she had to admit to a certain disappointment to hear it confirmed. "Ah, well," she said, "I have something more important to discuss in any case. I have worked out a little plan, and I need your assistance."

It took her what must have been a full half hour to persuade him to agree. He gave her every argument against her plan that he could think of, but she was adamant. "Once we have the proof, the inspector will have to listen to us," she insisted when Baxter pleaded with her to talk to the police first.

Finally he held up his hands in despair. "I can see you are determined," he said, "and I will not allow you to do this alone. But I feel very strongly that we are wasting our time. You are acting on supposition, and a frail one at that. On the other hand, there is always the possibility that you could very well be putting yourself in danger."

She leaned over and patted his arm. "That's why I need you there, Bax. I have every confidence in you. I shall feel perfectly safe knowing you are at my back, waiting to protect me."

"Yes, madam," he said gloomily.

Satisfied, she stood up. "Now, I have to go and get ready for dinner. You have it all straight?"

"Yes, madam."

"Good. Then I shall see you later."

As she turned away, she smiled when she heard him say under his breath, "And who in the world, may I ask, is going to protect me?"

CHAPTER

❊ 20 ❊

"I'm so glad you could join me," Cecily said, smiling at Daphne Morris across the table. The companion looked ill at ease, she thought, and wondered what was going through the woman's mind.

"It was most gracious of you to invite me," Miss Morris answered, picking at her lobster salad with her fish fork.

"Not at all. I enjoy having someone to talk to when I dine."

Daphne Morris looked up, and the candlelight accentuated the dark circles under her eyes. "You must miss your late husband a great deal."

Cecily nodded cheerfully. "I do, of course, but one can't go on pining away forever." She glanced around the crowded dining room, where ladies in elegant hats and frocks chattered and laughed with their immaculately dressed escorts. "After all, one can hardly be lonely, living in a hotel."

"Even in a crowded room, one can be terribly lonely if the right person is absent."

"True enough." She could almost feel sorry for the woman, Cecily thought, if it were not for her suspicions. "I imagine you will have to deal with loneliness as well, until you find a new position that is."

"Yes. I suppose I shall."

"Of course," Cecily said carefully, having led the conversation to where she needed it, "in view of the new developments, you might well have Mr. Danbury's help in finding new employment."

She felt a small leap of triumph when Daphne Morris sharply lifted her head. "Mr. Danbury? What developments?" Apparently aware that she had spoken too harshly, the companion added more quietly, "I am sorry, Mrs. Sinclair. But as you can understand, I am sure, I am naturally concerned in this matter."

"Of course, Miss Morris." Cecily lifted her serviette and dabbed at her lips. "I apologize for startling you, I assumed you had heard the news."

Daphne Morris laid down her fork with exaggerated care. "I am afraid I am unaware of any news of Mr. Danbury since he was taken away by the police this morning."

"Ah," Cecily said reaching for her wine. "Then let me enlighten you. Apparently there has been a new discovery at the scene of the murder."

"In the roof garden?"

Most clever, Cecily thought. It was obvious Daphne Morris had a very quick mind. "Oh, no, that is part of the news. The murder wasn't committed in the roof garden. Lady Eleanor was killed in the courtyard below. The fallen bricks from the roof were merely a decoy, in the hopes of making the death appear to be an accident."

Daphne Morris coughed and covered her mouth with her serviette.

"Are you all right, my dear?" Cecily inquired innocently.

The companion nodded, her eyes growing wary. "Thank you, I am fine. I find it so difficult to think of Mr. Danbury as

eing capable of such violence. I have always admired him as
 gentleman.''

"Ah, yes. Well, that is the other thing.'' Cecily sipped her
vine slowly. She was beginning to enjoy herself immensely.
'There appears to be some doubt of Mr. Danbury's involve-
nent in this affair after all. You see, the police uncovered a
white shoe button at the scene. Considering the place where it
vas found, it seems most likely that the button was lost during
he attack on Lady Eleanor.''

All color seemed to have drained from Daphne Morris's
ace. She took a hasty sip of her wine, choked, and set the glass
own again so hurriedly the liquid spilt on the white lace
ablecloth.

Dabbing at the stain with her serviette, Miss Morris mut-
ered, "I am so sorry, how clumsy of me.''

"Not at all. A discussion of murder can be most unnerving,
an it not?''

"Very.'' The younger woman appeared to recover herself in
ecord time. "So do the police have any notion of who might
e the owner of the button?''

Cecily shook her head. "Not for the time being. The
nspector informed me, however, that he would arrive very
arly tomorrow morning, before the guests are due to leave, so
hat they can inspect any white shoes the women might have.''

"White shoes?'' Daphne Morris whispered.

"Yes. It's a dreadful nuisance, of course. I'm afraid it will
e most awkward explaining to my guests why they have to
ubmit to this inspection, but I have no say in the matter. Of
ourse, since most of my staff wear white shoes . . .''

Cecily paused, as if she'd just thought of it. "Oh, dear, I'm
fraid that will include you, Miss Morris. If I remember, you
vere wearing white shoes with that charming white dress
esterday, were you not? I remember admiring them when we
isited in my suite. That network of straps was most novel, I
aven't seen a pair like that before.''

A red spot appeared in each of Miss Morris's cheeks. "Oh,
hank you. They were a gift from Lady Eleanor. Well, of
ourse I shall be happy to offer them for inspection in the
norning.''

"Wonderful," Cecily said, picking up her knife and fork. "I shall be sure to mention you to the inspector the moment he arrives. Perhaps he can see you first then you won't be delayed in leaving." With great enthusiasm, she attacked her ptarmigan pie.

"It went very well," Cecily quietly informed Baxter later. "Daphne Morris believed every word of it. I am quite sure that she is at this very moment racking her brains to find a solution to her dilemma."

"I am not happy with this situation at all, madam. There are several options Miss Morris can employ."

Cecily peered cautiously around the side of the laundry room. From there she had a clear view across the yard to the larder window. The sky had cleared, leaving only a few white clouds scudding across the moon. Pale white light flooded the ground, rendering anything that moved perfectly visible.

"Name one," she demanded without raising her voice.

"She could merely discard the shoes in a dustbin."

"I don't think so. I told her I remembered seeing her in them yesterday, and that I would ask the inspector to see her first."

"Most ingenious, madam. Perhaps Miss Morris has more than one pair of white shoes, however. In which case she would need only to present one pair to the inspector."

"I think not, since she was so anxious to replace the button yesterday. In any case, Baxter, these shoes were most distinctive. I'm quite sure I should recognize them again. Miss Morris knows that. No, I do believe that she will act precisely as I've predicted."

"And may I point out, madam, that if she does not, we could stand out here all night waiting for her?"

"Granted, that's entirely possible. But it's certainly worth the chance, is it not?"

Baxter cleared his throat several times and ran his finger under his collar.

Cecily looked at him suspiciously. "Is something distressing you, Baxter?"

"Madam, I have to remind you of the improprieties of being alone with a member of the . . . staff for the entire night."

Cecily grinned. "Don't you mean a member of the opposite sex, Bax? Isn't that what you were about to say?"

He shifted awkwardly on his feet. "Madam, I—"

"Oh, piffle. If we catch Miss Morris in the act, then our motives will be properly explained. If not, then no one but ourselves need know of this escapade. Agreed?"

"If you say so, madam."

"That's settled then. Now we had better keep quiet and hope that Daphne Morris is as predictable as I think she is."

Gertie was looking forward to putting her feet up. She'd been running all day and couldn't wait to get back to her room with a nice pot of tea and some of Mrs. Chubb's shortbread. She'd raided the kitchen after everyone had left and was scurrying along the hall to her room when she saw Daphne Morris standing in front of the housekeeper's sitting-room door.

Surprised, Gertie almost dropped her tea tray. "Blimey, miss, you gave me a right fright, you did. Is there something you wanted?"

The companion looked up and down the hall as if afraid a ghost were about to appear. "I was . . . er . . . just wondering if Mrs. Chubb was here? I wished to ask a favor of her."

Gertie shook her head. "Sorry, miss. It's her morning off tomorrow. She's gone to visit her daughter and the baby. She usually stays the night and comes back the next afternoon." It struck Gertie that Miss Morris looked right pasty, like she was ill.

"'Ere," Gertie said, peering at the wan face, "you feeling bad? I've got some powders in me room if you want one."

"Oh, no, thank you. I wanted to borrow a needle and cotton, but perhaps I'll wait until tomorrow."

"Sorry I can't help you with that one," Gertie said, shifting her grip on the tray. "Mrs. Chubb's the one who has all that. I can bring you some in the morning if you like."

Daphne Morris held up her hand. "No, no, thank you. It doesn't matter. Forget I mentioned it. Er . . . good night."

Gertie watched the tall, slender woman hurrying up the stairs to the lobby. Seemed odd that did, that she wouldn't have a needle and cotton. What kind of lady's companion came away without a needle and cotton? Shaking her head, Gertie carried the tray to her room.

"Madam, it is getting most chilly out here. I beg you—"

"Sshhsh!" Cecily pressed a finger to her lips. "I heard something." She edged her head forward until she could see around the corner.

For a moment nothing moved in the yard, then a dustbin lid rattled as a cat sprang to the ground and began prowling along the wall, tail held high in the air.

"Only a cat," Cecily whispered, withdrawing her head. "I thought—"

She stopped as another sound caught her ear. The faint creak of wood. Pushing her head forward again, Cecily peered around the corner. Her heart skipped when she saw the dark-clad figure crouching below the larder window.

Pulling back, she held out her hand. "It's her," she breathed. "Give me the helmet."

Baxter's eyes looked like silver in the moonlight. She thought he would argue and she stopped breathing, terrified that his voice would carry across the yard. But after a pause, he handed it to her.

Cecily waited a moment longer, then prepared herself and stepped out into the open.

Daphne Morris had her arm through the window, reaching inside.

Holding her breath, Cecily began walking toward her, her footsteps ringing out loudly in the still night air.

With a small cry, Miss Morris withdrew her arm and swung around.

Cecily stopped dead.

There was a small, shocked silence, then the companion clutched her throat. "Robert! What are you doing here? No, no, don't come any closer. Please, I didn't want to kill her. I thought it was what you wanted. I did it for you, Robert—"

Her voice broke and she sank to her knees, murmuring between sobs, "I . . . did . . . it . . . for . . . you."

Cecily removed her pith helmet. "I'm sorry, Miss Morris.

Mr. Danbury is not here. I just borrowed his uniform to wear, which is what you did last night, was it not?''

The sobs stopped abruptly as Daphne Morris peered across the yard. ''Mrs. Sinclair?''

''Yes.'' Cecily stepped out from the shadow of the wall into the moonlight. Her disguise had worked better than she could have hoped. ''I apologize for the deception,'' she added, ''but I needed confirmation that my suspicions were correct. I assume you were trying to reach the button tin, as you attempted to do last night, am I right? It was you who broke the pickle jar in your attempt to reach the button tin, I believe?''

Miss Morris stood very still. ''Button tin? I am sorry, I have no idea what you are talking about.''

''The button tin, Miss Morris. After you killed Lady Eleanor you realized the button was missing from your shoe. I saw those shoes myself this very afternoon, in your wardrobe. You must have considered the possibility of the button being found at the scene of the crime.''

She took a step forward. ''You knew about the button tin, of course. I'm sure you've had occasion to use it before. But you couldn't ask for it, could you? So you reached for it through the window. I imagine the noise of the falling jar must have been quite startling. Enough to cause you to leave at once, before you were discovered.''

For a long moment the silence stretched between them. Then, from the bushes nearby came the mournful yowl of a cat. Daphne Morris's eyes flickered in the pale light from the moon.

''You are too clever, Mrs. Sinclair,'' she said, her voice strident in the darkness. ''You would never have known, would you, if it hadn't been for that button? How very careless of me.''

Cecily stepped closer. ''You were in love with him, weren't you?''

The other woman stared at her, and Cecily could plainly see the fury in her eyes. ''Robert? Yes, I was in love with him. He swore he loved me, too. But he wouldn't divorce milady.''

''So you killed her.''

''I had to get rid of her so that he could be free.'' Her laugh rang out wildly. "Free! Can you imagine? I freed him all right, to walk into the arms of another woman. It was all for nothing."

"So you wrote the note, asking Lady Eleanor to meet you?"

Daphne Morris sighed. "Everything went wrong from the start. I intended to push her over the roof wall. I noticed the bricks were wearing, so I loosened them with Robert's paper knife. Then I shut Chan Ying in my wardrobe and sent Robert to look for him. I needed him out of the way. Then I suggested to Lady Eleanor that we should go to the roof to see if we could spy Chan Ying from up there."

Cecily stepped closer, intent on catching every soft-spoken word.

"Milady refused to go," Miss Morris continued, her hands writhing together like two battling snakes. "She said the staircase was too narrow. I had to think of something else. It was when I collected Robert's uniform that the idea came to me. It was a simple matter to pick up a mask from the reception desk and then I saw a helmet hanging on the hallstand. I changed into the clothes and scribbled the note and gave it to the maid."

"And then you met Lady Eleanor in the courtyard?"

Miss Morris looked confused. "Pardon? Oh, no. I waited in the roof garden and pushed the bricks down on her. I thought they would kill her. I hid the sign, so that people would think it was an accident, that perhaps someone had gone too close at the precise moment Lady Eleanor was taking a walk below."

It was Cecily's turn to be confused. "But I don't understand. Lady Eleanor wasn't killed by the falling bricks."

Daphne Morris gave a mirthless laugh. "So I discovered. I hurried down to the courtyard. I wanted to make sure she was quite dead. But she was still breathing when I reached her. I lifted a rock from the rockery, and she took hold of my foot. She must have regained consciousness and realized . . ."

The image was too much. Cecily suddenly felt a little dizzy. She took several deep breaths while Miss Morris simply stood there, staring at the ground.

"I think perhaps we should go inside," Cecily said, taking an unsteady step closer to the now silent woman.

Daphne Morris lifted her head, and now her eyes looked wild in the moonlight. "No! I shall not go to prison. I will not wait inside one of those terrible filthy holes while they decide whether or not to hang me. I will not!" Her voice rising on a howl, the demented woman rushed forward, heading straight at Cecily.

CHAPTER

❖ 21 ❖

Cecily stepped in front of the howling woman, arms outstretched, calling loudly, "Baxter!"

With a violent shove, Daphne Morris sent her sprawling, then rushed on.

Dazed for a moment, Cecily sat on the hard ground, then felt a pair of strong hands beneath her armpits, helping her to her feet.

"Madam, are you all right? Are you hurt?" Baxter's voice sounded gruff with anxiety.

"I am perfectly fine, thank you," Cecily said, feeling a little foolish. "But we must get after her, don't let her get away."

"I don't know where she would run to," Baxter said, but nevertheless began sprinting after the flying figure.

Doing her best to keep up, Cecily saw Daphne Morris plunge through the front door of the hotel with Baxter quite a distance behind her.

The manager's heavy bulk was no match for Miss Morris's athletic build, and he needed several moments to reach the door.

By the time Cecily had puffed her way up the steps at the fairly smart trot, both the companion and Baxter had disappeared from view.

Once inside the foyer, Cecily caught sight of her manager disappearing into the shadows around the curve of the staircase. Her heart seemed to stop beating. She had a terrible suspicion that she knew where Daphne Morris was going.

"Stop her!" she called out urgently and, hauling on the banister rail, began climbing the stairs two at a time. She knew in her heart that she couldn't possibly get there in time. She could only pray that Baxter could somehow find the speed to catch up with the poor woman.

Halfway up the second flight, she paused. Of course, the door to the roof was locked. But then Baxter had unlocked it for Ben Parkinson, the mason. Had he locked it again? She could only hope so. Once more she began climbing as fast as her aching legs would carry her.

Reaching the third floor at last, she stood for a moment on the landing, gasping for breath. It was a moment or two before she noticed, then her heart sank. The door leading to the roof garden stood wide open.

Very slowly, she walked toward it, and as she did so, Baxter appeared in the doorway, his face ashen in the glow from the gaslights.

"She jumped, didn't she?" Cecily asked breathlessly.

"Yes, madam. I am sorry. By the time I got there, she had already gone." He didn't wait for her answer, but dashed past her down the stairs.

Cecily followed much more slowly. There was no point in hurrying. She was quite certain that Daphne Morris could not possibly survive the fall.

She sat on the bottom step of the staircase, waiting for him to return. When he did, she could see by his set expression that there was nothing he could have done.

"She's dead?" she asked, though she already knew the answer.

"Yes. I am afraid so."

"Perhaps it's just as well."

Baxter shook his head. "If only I had locked the door. I had intended to, after Ben had finished with his calculations. Then Mrs. Chubb needed my assistance, and I had no time to go back before you and I were to meet. I intended to come back and lock it afterward. Now it is too late."

Cecily stood up. Patting his arm, she said quietly, "Baxter, please don't blame yourself. It is what she wanted, and you are in no way responsible for that."

He nodded, looking unconvinced. "We have to see that a message gets to Wellercombe."

"Of course." She rubbed her forehead, feeling suddenly exhausted. "This is yet another occasion when a telephone would have saved having to turn someone out in the middle of the night."

"It would have made no difference, madam, since the police station in Wellercombe is still on the telegraph system."

Cecily sighed. "True. I suppose it will take time for things to change down here."

"Yes, madam."

"We can't force those changes before their time, Baxter. Look at Daphne Morris. She thought she could win Robert Danbury, but he would never have married a lady's companion. Now that he has acquired a new station, Daphne Morris would have been considered beneath him. Maybe one day these things won't matter so much, and we can choose with whom we fall in love, without regard to whether or not it's a suitable match."

He didn't answer, and she sent a quick glance his way. As usual, his expression remained inscrutable.

"You know, Baxter," she said softly, "people worry too much much about the changing world. Here in the countryside, one would never know that technology has progressed at such a rapid rate. To all intents and purposes, Badgers End is still existing in the Dark Ages."

"I don't think that is necessarily a bad thing. Sometimes too rapid a change can bring new and unfamiliar problems with it."

"We have to live with the times, Baxter, whatever they might bring."

"I think we have to enjoy each day for itself, madam. If indeed the world is changing so rapidly, one might well consider that each tomorrow could bring unexpected catastrophes." He turned to walk down the hall.

She stared after him, uneasily aware that he could very well be right.

Inspector Cranshaw arrived early the next morning, with P.C. Northcott trotting on his heels, and immediately went to inspect the body. Cecily waited in the library, trying to remember everything clearly enough to answer the inevitable questions she knew would be fired at her.

Although Baxter had the morning off, he'd volunteered to stay and talk with the police, and she was most grateful for that.

As close as possible, she related the conversation she'd had with Daphne Morris the night before, with Baxter confirming everything she'd said.

Both the inspector and P.C. Northcott took notes this time, and Cecily gained some satisfaction from the fact that at last they were taking her seriously.

"It all seems straightforward enough," Inspector Cranshaw said after Cecily had answered his brief questions. "I will be in touch with you later, Mrs. Sinclair, if we need anything else from you."

He stood, and P.C. Northcott sprang to attention beside him. He reached for the inspector's hat and handed it to him with an anxious little flourish. Cranshaw took the hat without a word.

"I appreciate your cooperation in this matter," the inspector went on, fixing Cecily with his eagle stare, "but I must warn you about taking the law into your own hands. Had things not turned out the way you hoped, you would have been, and still might be, guilty of tampering with evidence in a murder case."

"I understand, Inspector," Cecily murmured, trying to sound contrite. "It won't happen again."

"I must also caution you," Cranshaw said sternly, "about stepping into situations that you are not qualified to handle.

This could have turned out very differently for you had Miss Morris been desperate enough to want to kill you.''

Cecily smiled. ''I had nothing to worry about, Inspector, with Baxter standing watch over me.''

The tall policeman seemed unimpressed. ''When dealing with the criminal mind, madam, we cannot count on anyone. The unpredictability and speed of such a person can be quite extraordinary. I must insist that in future, you leave such dangerous tasks to us. That is, after all, our job. We are trained professionals and, as such, are only hampered by amateurish meddling.''

''Quite, quite,'' P.C. Northcott muttered, staring at his superior with great admiration.

Cecily resisted the impulse to point out that had it not been for her amateurish meddling, they might never have discovered the real murderer. ''Inspector,'' she said, smiling sweetly up at him, ''I most sincerely hope that I shall not be afforded the opportunity for any more meddling. The Pennyfoot Hotel could not withstand such notoriety.''

''On that, madam, we most certainly agree.'' Inspector Cranshaw gave her a stiff little bow and left, followed at a respectable distance by P.C. Northcott.

Cecily looked at Baxter, who stood rocking on his heels. He still felt responsible for the death of Daphne Morris, she could tell. Knowing how upset he was, she didn't quite know what to say to comfort him. So she said the only thing possible at such a time. ''Come, Bax, let's go down to the kitchen and make ourselves a nice cup of tea.''

They reached the foyer, which was bustling with departing visitors, just as Robert Danbury arrived to collect his luggage. He looked pale and drawn, but he managed a curt smile when Cecily greeted him.

''I understand I have you to thank for my release,'' he said, lowering his voice as yet another couple descended the stairs. ''I am most grateful, Mrs. Sinclair. For everything.''

Cecily nodded. ''I hope, when the trauma of this has passed, we will see you again at the Pennyfoot?''

''I very much doubt it. Not that I haven't enjoyed my visits

here. But there would be too many ghosts to haunt me now."
He hesitated, then added "Tell me, where is Chan Ying?"

Surprised, Cecily looked up at him. "At the moment he is in
my housekeeper's sitting room, waiting for a friend of mine to
collect him. I thought you might not want to be bothered . . ."
Her voice trailed off when she saw the pain in his eyes.

"He is all I have left, Mrs. Sinclair. I would like to take him
home."

"Of course. I understand."

She felt a small glow when he answered, "Yes, I do believe
you do."

He turned away, and she looked back at Baxter, who stood
staring at the staircase with the oddest expression on his face.
Following his gaze, Cecily saw the couple reach the bottom
step and smile at each other.

The lady she didn't recognize. The gentleman, however,
seemed startlingly familiar. He was short and very stout with a
neat white beard and rather unbecoming bulging eyes.

Mesmerized by the couple, Cecily watched them cross the
foyer, followed by a flurry of footmen and luggage, then
disappear out of the door.

Slowly she turned to Baxter, who just as slowly turned
toward her. For several long moments they stared at each other.
Then Cecily dispersed the cobwebs from her mind with a firm
shake of her head. "No," she said firmly, "it couldn't have
been His Majesty. Could it?"

Looking her straight in the eye Baxter replied, "Of course
not, madam. I heard that King Edward is on the continent,
taking the cure."

Cecily nodded. "That's what I thought. Though the man
looked remarkably like him, I must say."

"Remarkably." He turned away, leaving her staring suspiciously after him.

By Monday evening Ben had finished repairing the wall, and
once more Cecily could stand looking out over the cove to the
horizon beyond. There were no clouds to mar the sky, and a
clear, aquamarine sea gently lapped at the sands.

The hotel was fairly quiet, the bulk of the guests having

returned to the city, leaving no more than a dozen or so visitors to enjoy the peace and quiet. By midweek the tumult would begin again, but for now, the respite was most welcomed by the hotel staff.

Out of habit, Cecily reached for a rosebud, then pulled back her hand. No more. She had promised herself she would not dwell on her grief anymore. She would fill her life with the hotel, and whatever good work she could do in the village. Phoebe was always asking for her help at various functions.

It was time she got out more, Cecily decided. It would be most comforting to feel needed again.

The door opened behind her, and she turned to see Baxter stepping through. He seemed relieved when he saw her.

"Mrs. Chubb told me you had come up here." His gaze wandered to the wall. "I was a little concerned—"

"Baxter!" Cecily exclaimed. "Surely you didn't think—"

"No, madam, of course not."

The shock on his face made her laugh. "Then tell me what you were so concerned about."

"I know the reason you enjoy being up here, and I thought perhaps, after everything that has happened, you might be distressed . . ."

His voice faded away. Then, as she continued to look at him, he added lamely, "I thought perhaps it had spoilt things for you, madam."

Touched by his perception, Cecily smiled. "It might have, Baxter, if I hadn't decided that I've mourned long enough. I shall still cherish my memories, of course, but I'm no longer governed by them."

He looked as if he didn't know how to answer her, and she changed the subject. "Has Colonel Fortescue left yet? I haven't seen him today."

"Yes, madam. With assurances that he will return in a week or two."

Cecily nodded. "No doubt." She turned back to look out at the ocean. "I was talking to him, you know, when everything fell into place."

"Yes, madam?"

"If it hadn't been for Henry being disturbed and all the

ramifications that followed, I might never have stumbled on the truth. It never occurred to me that it could have been a woman who gave the note to Gertie. Until the colonel started chattering about the uproar caused by Henry, and that he hadn't realized the sultan was a woman." She smiled. "You know he actually thought it was all part of the performance?"

"He would be most gratified to know that he was such a help."

Cecily smiled. "Yes, he would, wouldn't he? It's so strange how everything became linked together. First the plants, which made me realize that rocks had to have been moved. I wonder why John didn't think of that?"

"John's mind was on the plants themselves, I believe. Not the rocks. He apparently assumed they had been torn out by someone's hand."

"Yes, I suppose that had to be it. I do believe the button came off Miss Morris's shoe when Lady Eleanor clutched her foot." She shuddered. "That must have been a dreadful moment for that poor woman. Imagine recovering consciousness only to find Miss Morris poised above her with a jagged rock in her hands."

"Indeed so. The button apparently fell into the hole without Miss Morris noticing it."

"Then she replaced the rock on top of it. It wasn't until later she realized it was missing. Perhaps she went back to look for it, then when she couldn't find it, decided she would have to replace it, in case it was found."

Cecily placed her hands on the wall and looked down at the Esplanade. The shadows made by the railings were growing long. Soon the sky would turn peach, then pink and finally purple, before giving in to the night. "It must have been Miss Morris who overturned the plant pot," she said, gazing out across the ocean. "Can you imagine her panic as she raced down those stairs to make sure Lady Eleanor was dead?"

Baxter moved to stand next to her. "I wonder what it is that makes a woman so desperate she is ready to kill for a man."

Cecily glanced up at his expressionless face. "Love, Baxter. Some women love so desperately they will do anything to win the man they adore. Maybe it is a good thing that men are not capable of loving that madly.''

Baxter looked down at her. "Surely you are mistaken? I have heard of men driven to distraction by love for a woman. Think of the thousands of duels that have been fought over women.''

"Maybe so, Bax, maybe so. But men do not kill their rivals to win the love of a woman. They kill to prove their superiority and claim their prize. There is a great difference there.''

"I do believe you are becoming a cynic, madam.''

"I certainly hope not.'' She looked back at the cliffs dominating the skyline. "In spite of what Miss Morris did, I can't help feeling sympathetic. She must have loved him very much to commit such a terrible act.''

"And it was wasted. He has another lover.''

"But he's not in love. Robert Danbury loved his wife. I truly believe that. It was the reason I found it so hard to believe he had killed her. I think Lady Eleanor married him out of spite toward Keith Torrington and had no real love for him. But he loved her. The other women were a poor substitute for the attention he craved from his wife.''

"You surprise me, madam. First a cynic, now a romantic. What made you so certain Mr. Danbury loved his wife?''

Cecily sighed. "The look in his eyes when he saw her dead body. For just a moment I saw anger there. I know where that anger comes from. It happens when you lose someone you love very much. It is a senseless rage burning inside you, first against the person you loved for leaving you alone, and then against the fates that took them away. I know that feeling well.''

Baxter was quiet for a long time beside her, then he murmured, "Would you prefer to be alone, madam?''

She shook her head. Looking out toward the lighthouse she said, "I hear they will be coming to build a new lighthouse soon. They say they will install a single beam to replace the arc lights. A beam so powerful it will be seen more than ten miles out to sea. A comforting thought, no doubt, for those lost in a storm.''

"As I said, madam, not all changes are detrimental.''

She laughed and turned her face to look up at him. "You know, Baxter, I confess I'm going to find things quite dull around here after all this excitement."

"Yes, madam."

She smiled, hearing the unspoken relief in his voice. "Baxter," she said, with a mischievous grin, "please may I have one of your cigars?"

To her astonishment, he handed her one without another word.

SPECIAL PREVIEW!

If you enjoyed the adventures of Cecily Sinclair,
turn the page for a sneak preview of the next
Pennyfoot Hotel mystery. . .

DO NOT DISTURB

A mysterious murder by poison points to Cecily's friend
Madeline as a suspect. Cecily takes on the job to clear her
friend's name and hunt down the real culprit!

Look for **DO NOT DISTURB**
by Kate Kingsbury,
coming from Jove Books
in January 1994!

❀ ❀ ❀

The summer of 1906 had been cool and damp in England. Nevertheless, autumn came slowly to the village of Badgers End and its sheltered cove on the southeast coast.

The season began with a crisp, clean chill in the breeze from the English Channel and a tinge of gold to the willow leaves that hung over Deep Willow Pond. Acrid smoke curled from chimney pots and drifted lazily across Putney Downs, and the sun threw long shadows a little earlier each day.

Hawthorne Lane crossed the Downs in a meandering trail of hedgerows and wildflowers, barely leaving room for the cart horses pulling their loads to market. Usually the lane became deserted by sundown, except for the stray rabbit or inquisitive hedgehog.

This evening, however, as dusk seeped over the countryside, four grubby-faced urchins dressed in shabby knickerbockers stole along the lane, one behind the other.

A muffled giggle disturbed the quiet peace, and the leader of the group twisted his head with an urgent, ''Sshhh!''

''Shut up, you blithering idiots,'' someone else whispered, and the laughter was suppressed.

The straggly line continued in silence, except for the occasional scrape of a boot against the surface of the road. Soon the boys reached a row of six cottages and could look down from their lofty perch to the dark blue cove below with its crescent of golden sand.

Hidden by the tall hedges that lined the bottom of the gardens, they conferred with hand signals. Then each of them chose a garden path and crept silently up to the front door. Quickly each boy tied one end of thick cotton thread to the door knocker, then scuttled back to the shelter of the hedges.

The leader of the group, a tough-looking redhead with protruding ears, lifted his hand. Four fists clutched four lengths of thread, trembling with anticipation.

The signaling hand fell, and four fists jerked at once. The door knockers clattered in a cacophony of sound, setting off a furious chorus of barking dogs.

Four doors opened as if on cue, one after the other. After a short pause, three men and a woman stepped onto their porches, looking across at each other in bewilderment.

With a loud snort of uncontrolled laughter, one of the boys raced down the lane, followed by his three companions, all with fists shoved in their mouths to curb the sound of their glee.

Looking after them, the woman said sharply, ''Those boys and that stupid game. Ought to know better, they did.'' Her neighbors shook their heads and, amid muttered curses, returned to their fireplaces. Peace settled once more over Hawthorne Lane.

The sun gradually sank out of sight, abandoning the sky to the moon. The shadows merged, softened, and reappeared, bathed in a ghostly pale light.

A man walked steadily along the lane, from the direction of the cove. In spite of the steep climb, his breathing sounded even in the shrouded silence of the Downs.

The cottages were in darkness, the inhabitants having succumbed to the weariness of long hours in the fields. The man strode past them all until he reached the last one in the row.

After turning into the path, he walked firmly up to the front door, opened it with a key, and disappeared inside.

Some time later, a single rap of a door knocker once more disturbed the peace in the lane. This time the summons had been served on the door of the end cottage.

The man inside cursed. He had just snuggled down in his bed, his hot water bottle nestled at his feet. He was inclined to ignore the knock, in the hopes that whoever it was would go away.

But he couldn't. There was always the possibility that it could be someone from the work site, some problem that needed his immediate attention.

Muttering to himself, the man found the oil lamp in the dark and struck a match. In the flickering light he dragged the eiderdown from the bed and wrapped it around his shoulders. His feet were cold again, and he thought longingly of the hot water bottle as he opened the door. No one was there.

Frowning, he leaned forward, peering into the darkness. Surely he hadn't imagined the knock? He thought he heard a slight sound, a soft movement in the shadows. He stepped outside for a better look. Still he could see nothing but the outline of the hedges against the dark sky.

The eiderdown slipped from his shoulders, and he caught it, turning impatiently back to the warmth of the cottage. Something touched his neck, and he lifted a hand to explore. He took a couple of steps, then blinked. His eyelids felt curiously heavy. He hadn't realized how desperately tired he felt—so tired he couldn't lift his eyelids again.

He couldn't open his eyes. He felt odd; his face seemed stiff, his jaw tight. He tried to grimace, but his mouth wouldn't move. His chin dropped, and try as he might he couldn't lift his head.

Panic rose, swift and terrifying, as he staggered, one hand groping for the door frame. He couldn't swallow. His lungs felt as though they were gripped in a steel vice, tightening, tightening. . . .

The pain was terrible. His legs buckled, writhing in agony, while the top half of him seemed frozen solid. He couldn't breathe

. . . the awful agony of it . . . he twitched violently . . . then lay still.

By mid-morning Cecily Sinclair had finished her rounds of the gardens and sat relaxing in the library of the Pennyfoot Hotel, awaiting the arrival of Phoebe Carter-Holmes and Madeline Pengrath, the members of her entertainment committee.

Although the waning of the season meant a lull in the social activities at the hotel, Cecily still liked to arrange something for the few guests who chose to visit the tiny seaside town during the quieter months.

The cool, mellow autumn days always brought a special feeling of pleasurable relief after the hectic weeks of summer. The Pennyfoot had gained a considerable reputation as a unique and elegant retreat for the jaded upper class of the big city.

From May to September its rooms were filled, enjoyed by the elite in their pursuit of pleasure, safe in the knowledge that their indiscretions would be kept secret by the remarkably discreet staff of the hotel.

James Sinclair, Cecily's late husband, had chosen his employees with the utmost care, leaving each of them in no doubt of their fate should they ever breathe one word of the goings-on behind the Pennyfoot's sedate white walls.

It was a measure of the staff's loyalty that no word of scandal had ever touched the name of the Pennyfoot Hotel. Cecily was very proud of that. And now that her beloved James was gone, taken by the malaria he'd contracted while serving in Her Majesty's Service in the tropics, Cecily was more determined than ever that his legacy be maintained in the manner he had dictated.

That was the main reason Cecily had taken over some of the duties as owner of the hotel. The renovations James had undertaken still left heavy debts, and Cecily was determined to keep the hotel in the family, as James had requested at his death.

Seated at the head of the long mahogany table, Cecily glanced up at her husband's portrait hanging over the huge marble fireplace. At forty-three, she was much too young to be a widow, she thought sadly. Who would have imagined, when James first acquired what had once been the family home of the Earl of Saltchester, that a few short years later he would die, much too soon, leaving her to carry on alone?

The paneled door opened, cutting short her reverie. A very large hat appeared, loaded down with ostrich feathers, with a swathe of cream chiffon enveloping huge bronze and dark red chrysanthemums. The middle-aged face underneath it smiled, while a pair of bright blue eyes gazed across the room.

"Cecily, dear, am I late? I'm so sorry. Algie was fussing over his sermon for Sunday and insisted I listen to it. Sometimes I wonder what he'd do if I weren't around to hold his hand. There can't be many vicars who have a mother willing to spend so much time helping them with their work."

Cecily smiled back. "Come in, Phoebe. No, you're not late. I came in early. It's getting a little cool to stay out in the gardens too long in the mornings. The sea breeze can be very fresh."

The hat nodded vigorously, threatening to overbalance had it not been securely pinned. "I know exactly what you mean. I shall have to dig out my winter coats and muffs before the east wind gets a bite to it."

The door opened again and a willowy woman dressed in pale mauve muslin swept in. Long dark hair flowed free and settled about her shoulders, and her expressive dark eyes flitted about the room, never still.

"My goodness," she murmured in a low, whispery voice that always reminded Cecily of windblown rushes, "I do declare, the evil spirits are about in force today. I can feel them all around me."

"Oh, for heaven's sake, Madeline, please don't start that again," Phoebe complained, carefully smoothing her green silk skirt as she sat on the padded chair behind the table.

Madeline paused long enough to give Phoebe a disdainful sniff before floating over to a chair on the opposite side of the table, in front of the massive bookshelves. Shaking her hair back from her face with a toss of her head, she looked at Cecily. "At least you have the good sense to take heed of what I say."

Cecily shifted uncomfortably on her chair. It was true that Madeline had an uncanny knack for sensing trouble. In fact, Madeline had a certain strange aptitude for all kinds of things.

Her talent for healing various ailments with potions concocted from plants grown in her abundant garden caused much speculation among the villagers. Half of them swore that Madeline's potions worked far better than anything the doctor could prescribe, while the other half were convinced that they'd be possessed by demons if they so much as touched a leaf from one of her plants.

The fact of the matter was, Madeline had earned the dubious reputation of being, at best, a gypsy changeling, and at worst, a witch. The woman's appearance went a long way toward fostering that belief.

Although Cecily was quite sure that Madeline was close to her own age, the woman's gleaming black hair revealed not a single strand of gray, and her skin was as smooth and soft as a young woman of twenty.

Compared to Madeline, Cecily felt positively ancient, what with her sensible light brown chignon sprinkled with silver and the deep laughter lines at the corners of her eyes.

"Well," Phoebe said, opening her handbag to pull out a lace-edged handkerchief, "I'm quite sure your evil spirits are nothing more than those little hooligans running around playing that Knock Down Ginger. Such an annoying game. I'm so tired of answering my door to thin air, and Algie swears his nerves have been shattered by the little devils."

"Algie's nerves can be shattered by a sneeze," Madeline said dryly.

Sensing the usual confrontation between the two women, Cecily launched into a discussion of the tea dance planned for that week.

Madeline, who took care of all the floral arrangements, outlined her ideas, and Phoebe, as entertainments director, described the women's violin quartet she'd hired. The details had just been finalized when a smart tap sounded on the door. All three heads turned toward the sound as Cecily called out, "Yes, come in."

The tall, broad-shouldered man who entered wore a worried

frown on his pleasant features. "Please excuse the intrusion, madam, but I thought you should know right away. We have a small problem in the bathrooms."

Cecily regarded her manager with anxious eyes. Baxter never consulted her unless the matter was serious. "What kind of problem?" she asked warily.

"I'm afraid it is a plumbing problem, madam. We shall have to close the bathrooms down until it is taken care of. I have sent for the plumber, but he is in Wellercombe at the moment, and it could be some time before he arrives. I felt that you should be informed."

Cecily raised her eyebrows. "All three bathrooms?"

"All three." Baxter lifted his hands in a helpless gesture. "I'm sorry, madam."

"Yes, well, I'm sure it's not your fault. Thank you, Baxter."

Instead of leaving, Baxter remained where he was, an odd expression on his face.

Cecily frowned. "Was there something else?"

"I wasn't sure if you'd heard, madam. About the foreman of the lighthouse project?"

Madeline sat up straight as Cecily continued to gaze at her manager. "What about the foreman, Baxter?"

"He's dead, madam. They found him lying outside his cottage this morning. Apparently he died of a heart attack."

Since Cecily didn't know the man in question personally, Baxter's news wasn't all that startling. What was startling was Madeline's reaction to it. With a strangled cry she leapt to her feet, one hand clutching her throat. Then, without a word she fled from the room, leaving the rest of the occupants staring after her in surprise.

"Well!" Phoebe exclaimed, fluttering her handkerchief in front of her face, "Whatever is the matter with her, I do wonder?"

Cecily privately wondered the same thing, though all she said was, "You know how sensitive Madeline is. She is devastated if she finds a dead bird."

"A dead bird, yes." Phoebe sniffed. "However, I have yet to see Madeline display such lavish emotion over a human being. Until now, that is." Luckily the more macabre details of

Baxter's announcement held more interest for her, and she added, "Will he be buried here, do you think? It has been a while since Algie had a funeral. I do so enjoy funerals."

Baxter raised his eyebrows. Catching Cecily's gaze, he rolled his eyes to the ceiling in an expression of disbelief.

Phoebe, who had her back to him, gushed on. "Not that I like to see people die, of course, but once they are dead, I mean, there's not much you can do about it, can you? You might as well enjoy the send-off, as I'm sure they would also, if—"

"Mrs. Carter-Holmes," Baxter interrupted, in a rare display of impropriety, "I do believe Mrs. Chubb was looking for you. I told her I would inform you at the earliest opportunity."

For a moment Phoebe looked affronted at this rude intrusion into her conversation, but then curiosity got the better of her. "Did she say what she wanted?" she asked, getting up from her chair with a rustle of silk.

"I'm afraid not."

"Ah, well, then, I had better go and find out for myself. Thank you, Mr. Baxter." She reached the door and looked back. "Oh, Cecily I very nearly forgot. I would like to discuss the church bazaar with you, if you have time this afternoon? Perhaps you could meet me in Dolly's Teashop? About three o'clock?"

Cecily smiled. "Of course, Phoebe. I'd be happy to meet you."

"Fine. Then I will see you later."

The door closed behind her, barely preceding Baxter's exasperated grunt. "That woman," he muttered darkly, "has the sensitivity of a wild boar."

In spite of herself, Cecily had to laugh. "She means well. She doesn't always think before she speaks, but her heart is in the right place."

He made a sound of disgust. "I do not understand how she could prattle on like that. Surely she hasn't forgotten whose funeral was the last one to be held at St. Bartholomew's?"

Touched by his concern, she said gently, "It's all right, Baxter. It's been almost ten months, after all."

"If I might be permitted to point out, madam, that is not a

long time for the pain to fade. To be reminded so irreverently of your loss must be most distressing.''

"James would not want me to be miserable on his behalf for too long.'' She glanced down at her hands to hide the sudden surge of emotion that could still catch her unawares. "I'm quite sure Phoebe would be horrified if she thought she'd caused me any anguish.''

"Perhaps. However, I do wish the woman would watch her tongue.''

"Oh, come now, Baxter. Life would be very dull without friends like Phoebe. She can be most entertaining at times.''

Baxter looked down his nose. "So I assume. Mr. Rawlins seems quite taken with her, though I can't imagine why.''

Cecily looked at him in astonishment. "Mr. Rawlins? I wasn't aware that he'd met Phoebe.'' A mental picture formed in her mind of the short, frail figure of the artist who had booked into the hotel the day before. With his flowing locks, huge dark eyes and pallid complexion, he reminded her of the statue of Jesus hanging above the alter in St. Bartholomew's.

"Mr. Rawlins caught sight of Mrs. Carter-Holmes this morning and enquired as to her name. When I informed him, he seemed quite disappointed, until I mentioned the fact that she was a widow. At that he brightened considerably. He asked me to introduce him at the first opportunity.''

"Really,'' Cecily murmured. "How intriguing. They are around the same age, of course. But I wouldn't have thought. . . .'' She let the sentence trail off. She knew only too well what it was like to be lonely.

"Madam?''

She looked up to see a hint of concern in Baxter's light gray eyes. She smiled. "No matter. I hope you will engineer an introduction as soon as possible. It will do Phoebe a world of good.''

Baxter's expression portrayed his extreme doubts, but he refrained from answering.

Cecily decided it was time to change the subject. "Now, tell me more about this poor man who died,'' she demanded.

"I'm afraid I know very little about it. The postman told me the news. He was up at Hawthorne Cottages when they took the poor devil away. Only a young chap, so the postman said. Couldn't have been thirty.''

"Oh, how awful. His poor family." Cecily glanced up at James's portrait. She knew how it was to lose a beloved one before his time. She'd expected him to go on living forever. Certainly into old age, in any case.

"I wonder if Madeline knew the foreman," she added, remembering the woman's sudden dash from the room. "She seemed very upset at the news."

"I assume that she had some acquaintance with him," Baxter said delicately.

Cecily sighed. They both knew quite well Madeline's reputation for befriending strangers. Most of the rumors, Cecily felt sure, were misconstrued. Of course, Madeline's private life was her own concern and nobody else's, but Cecily couldn't help wishing her friend was a little more prudent in her choice of companionship. Something told her that this time Madeline could have made a serious mistake.